The Man in The Glass Office

OrangeBooks Publication

1st Floor, Rajhans Arcade, Mall Road, Kohka, Bhilai, Chhattisgarh 490020
Website: **www.orangebooks.in**

First Edition, 2026

ISBN: 978-93-7426-166-8

Price: Rs. 260.00

Printed in India

THE MAN IN THE GLASS OFFICE

A STORY OF FINDING HOME

DR VIKASH AGARWAL

OrangeBooks Publication
www.orangebooks.in

Dedication

For Papa and Maa Neha Shlok.

You were my umbrella in the rain, long before I knew how to hold one.

The real voyage of discovery consists not in seeking new landscapes, but in having new eyes.

— MARCEL PROUST

Acknowledgments

This book is a work of fiction, but the journey it describes is real. It is a journey I could not have made alone.

To my own "Maya," who first handed me a mirror and had the patience to wait until I had the courage to look. You know who you are. This book is an echo of your wisdom.

To my family, my own "Neha" and "Shlok," who have been my greatest teachers. You are my most important "mud," my deepest anchor, and my reason for coming home. Thank you for your boundless patience as I learned to put down my armor and just be present.

To my team, You are the engineers and partners who co-created these new ways of working with me. Your courage to speak the truth, even when it was hard, is the real "New Covenant."

And finally, to you, the reader. If you picked up this book, you are likely on a journey of your own. You are not alone. The glass office is an illusion, and the mud is where real life is waiting. May you find your anchor.

Table of Contents

Introduction
The Invisible Wall

There is a specific kind of loneliness that comes with success.

We often imagine that as we climb the corporate ladder, we will gain more freedom, more control, and more clarity. We work 80-hour weeks, sacrifice weekends, and obsess over metrics, believing that once we reach the "corner office," we will finally feel safe.

But for many leaders, the opposite happens.

As we rise, the walls around us do not disappear; they just turn to glass. We become highly visible. Everyone watches us—our team, our board, our clients. They look to us for answers, for direction, and for strength. We are on display, perfectly transparent, yet completely isolated.

This is the "Glass Office." It is a state where we are seen by everyone but truly known by no one.

Inside this glass office, a silent epidemic is spreading. It is the epidemic of high-functioning anxiety. It is the "roommate" in our head that wakes us up at 3:00 AM, replaying a conversation from yesterday or catastrophizing a meeting for tomorrow. It is the exhausting effort of performing the role of the "perfect leader" while internally feeling like we are one mistake away from being exposed as a fraud.

I wrote this book because I have spent my career operating at the intersection of financial discipline and human potential. As a Chartered Accountant (CA) and a Doctor of Business Administration (DBA), I have spent decades analyzing what makes businesses succeed or fail.

We spend billions of dollars auditing our financial balance sheets. We track every penny of profit and loss. Yet, we spend almost zero time auditing the hidden liability that kills performance faster than any market downturn: The Anxiety Tax.

The Anxiety Tax is the cost of fear. It is the productivity lost when a manager is too afraid to speak up. It is the creativity killed when a team hides their mistakes instead of fixing them. It is the burnout that happens when a leader tries to be a "hero" instead of a human being.

This book is a fable, but it is not fiction. Ben Harris, the protagonist, is a composite of the hundreds of brilliant, exhausted leaders I have worked with. His journey—from the performative perfection of the Glass Office to the messy, resilient reality of "The Mud"—is the journey we all must make if we want to lead in the modern world.

You do not need to be a "guru" to lead a high-performing team. You do not need to be a stoic robot who never feels fear. You just need to learn a few simple tools to quiet the noise, anchor yourself in the present, and build a culture where it is safe to tell the truth.

As you read Ben's story, you may recognize his "roommate." You may recognize his fear. My hope is that, by the end, you will also recognize his freedom.

Welcome to the 41st floor.

Dr. Vikash Agarwal

Chapter - 1
The Roommate Who Never Shuts Up

Ben Harris had the corner office on the 41st floor. The city of London sprawled beneath him, a map of his own success. To the junior associates who walked by, their reflections sliding across the glass walls of his office, Ben was a goal. A partner by 38. A sharp suit, a sharper mind. He was, by every external measure, a man who had won.

But inside the glass office, Ben was losing.

He was in the middle of a 20-million-pound proposal, but his mind was in three other places at once.

- *...did I remember to reply to Johnson's email? God, his last email was so passive-aggressive. He's trying to poach the account, I know it...*
- *...stomach feels tight. Too much coffee. Need to cut back. Maybe I'll start that diet on Monday. I said that last Monday...*
- *...that argument with Hannah this morning. Why did I say that? She's right, I'm never present. But she doesn't understand the pressure, this...*

"Ben?"

Ben snapped back. His heart gave a painful jolt. Sarah, the division head, was looking at him from the head of the conference table. The entire executive team was on the video call, their faces a gallery of impatient pixels.

"Your take on the liability clause?" Sarah asked, her voice dangerously neutral.

Ben's mind was a blank, white screen. He had been so lost in the screaming chaos of his own thoughts that he hadn't just missed the question—he had no idea what *topic* they were on. He could feel the hot flush creep up his neck.

"Absolutely," he said, his voice a half-octave too high. He bought himself three seconds by shuffling the papers in front of him, his mind racing. *Liability... liability... what client was this?*

It was a nightmare. He was the expert, the one who was supposed to be ten steps ahead. But for the last six months, he'd been hollow. He was a brilliant actor playing the part of "Ben Harris," but the real Ben was gone, lost in a fog of anxiety, to-do lists, and a vague, crushing sense of dread.

He fumbled through an answer. It was just good enough. The meeting moved on. But the mask had slipped. He'd seen the look of concern, or was it pity, in Sarah's eyes.

The call came two hours later.

"Ben," Sarah's voice was firm, not unkind. "You weren't in that meeting."

"Sarah, I'm sorry, I was just..."

"Don't," she cut him off. "I'm not angry. I'm concerned. You're our top guy, but you're running on fumes. The firm is investing in you. We're booking you a session with a performance coach."

Ben felt a surge of humiliation. "A coach? Like a therapist?"

"No," Sarah said. "She's... different. She works with top-tier executives. Not on strategy. On focus. It's mandatory, Ben. Your first session is tomorrow."

The calendar invite popped up before he could even reply. "Introductory Session: Dr. Maya Aris."

Ben hung up the phone and stared out the glass. He felt like a fraud. A man who had everything, but who couldn't even manage to be in his own life. He was trapped in his own head, and the terrifying part was that he had no idea how to get out.

He had an inescapable, invisible roommate in his head, and it was screaming so loudly he could no longer hear his own life. He didn't just need to focus. He needed to be saved.

Chapter - 2
The Two-Word Question

The address Sarah had given him was not in the sterile, steel-and-glass forest of the financial district. It was a small, unmarked door of dark green wood, tucked away in a quiet cobblestone alley in Marylebone.

Ben checked his watch. 10:00 AM. He was used to meetings that started at 7 AM. This felt… civilized. He straightened his tie, a purely reflexive gesture, and pushed the door.

There was no receptionist. Just a small, quiet waiting room with two comfortable chairs and a simple, elegant plant. It smelled faintly of old books and green tea. This was not the office of a "performance coach." There were no framed posters of eagles soaring over mountains with words like "SUCCESS" or "LEADERSHIP."

"Mr. Harris?"

He turned. A woman stood in a doorway he hadn't noticed. She wasn't what he expected. She was in her late fifties, perhaps, with a kind, unlined face and intelligent, dark eyes that seemed to see everything. She wore simple linen trousers and a soft, gray sweater. She wasn't a "Dr." or a "coach." She looked like someone's brilliant, slightly eccentric aunt.

"Ben, please," he said, extending a hand.

"Maya," she replied, shaking his hand. Her grip was firm and warm. "Come in. Tea?"

"Coffee," Ben said automatically. "Black."

"We'll have tea," she said with a gentle smile that was somehow not a negotiation. "It'll be better for this conversation."

Her office was just as simple. Two armchairs, a low table, and a wall of books. No desk. No computer. It was the least intimidating room he had ever been in, and it put him completely on edge.

He sat, his body a stiff, formal line. He decided to take control of the meeting.

"Dr. Aris," he began, "I should be clear. I'm here because my firm insisted. I've had a minor... a temporary... dip in focus. My workload has increased substantially, and I'm sure you understand, in a high-pressure M&A environment, the cognitive load can be..."

Maya held up a hand. It was not an interruption, but a pause.

"Ben," she said, her voice soft but with a kind of clear, bell-like resonance. "Who just said all that?"

Ben blinked. The question was so absurd, it short-circuited his brain.

"I... I did, of course."

"Are you sure?" she asked, leaning forward, her eyes full of genuine, un-judging curiosity. "Or was it the part of you I'll call your 'Publicist'? The one whose job it is to manage the story, to make sure everyone in the room knows you are competent, in control, and definitely not the kind of man who needs help."

Ben's mouth opened, but nothing came out. He felt like a fish that had just been pulled from the water.

"Let's try again," Maya said gently. She poured him a cup of tea. It smelled like jasmine. "Forget the proposal, forget Sarah, forget the firm. Tell me, Ben, what is it like to be you... in there?" She tapped her own temple.

He tried to laugh it off, but the sound was hollow. "It's... busy. It's a busy place."

"Busy?" she smiled. "Or is it a warzone? Is it like having the world's most critical, most anxious, most relentless roommate living inside your skull? The one who tells you that you're a fraud when you fail, and that you just got lucky when you succeed? The one who is screaming at you about an email from yesterday while you're trying to have a conversation with your wife, and then screams at you for not listening to your wife?"

Ben stopped breathing. The silence in the room was absolute. He stared into his teacup, seeing not the tea, but the reflection of his entire, frantic, hollow life.

"Yes," he said, his voice barely a whisper. "That's it. Exactly. He never, ever shuts up."

"I know," Maya said, her voice full of a deep, uncomplicated empathy that nearly broke him. "And you have been at war with him for so long, you think you *are* him. You think that frantic, critical voice is... Ben."

"It's not?" The question sounded childish, but it was the most honest thing he'd said in a decade.

"No," she said. "It's not. The real you is the one who is listening to him. The real you is the one who is exhausted. The real you is the one who is sitting in this chair, hearing me, and feeling, for the first time in a long time, a tiny flicker of hope."

She leaned in. "Our work together is not to make that roommate 'focus.' You can't train a madman. Our work is to do something much more simple, and much more radical. We are going to learn to stop believing everything he says."

"How?" Ben asked. "How do you do that?"

"For now," Maya said, "you don't. For this week, your only job is to notice him. That's all. You're a detective. When you catch your mind spiraling... when you hear that roommate shouting about a deadline or replaying an argument... I want you to just silently, gently, label it. Just two words."

She held up two fingers.

"What two words?" Ben asked.

"Thinking," she said. "That's all. Not 'my thoughts,' which gives you ownership. Not 'this is a disaster.' Just... 'Thinking.' You are not the thoughts. You are the one who is noticing the thinking. That's the first step to freedom. Go notice."

Chapter - 3
The Man Who Wasn't There

Saturday morning. Ben was, by all reasonable definitions, not at work. He was in his beautiful, sun-drenched kitchen, wearing an expensive athleisure hoodie. The coffee in his hand was from a small-batch roaster. His life was a curated magazine spread.

And he was miserable.

He was staring at his phone, his thumb flicking through market analyses. His mind wasn't in the kitchen. It was on Monday. It was on the Johnson account. It was on the subtle, imagined condescension in a rival partner's last email.

"Want to take Leo to the park?"

Ben didn't look up. "Hmm? Yeah, in a bit, Han. Just need to get through this."

Hannah, his wife, stood by the counter. She had been bright and loving when they first met. Now she looked... tired. She had the resigned, quiet patience of a woman who has learned to expect to be the second priority, even on a weekend.

She didn't sigh. She didn't argue. She just said, "Okay," and the silence that followed was heavy and cold.

Ben felt a familiar, dull ache. Guilt. Followed immediately by its twin: defensiveness. *She doesn't get it. This is what it takes. This is for us.*

Then, a new voice. Maya's. *Who just said all that?*

Ben flinched. He put his phone face-down on the cold marble countertop. He was supposed to be a detective. He was supposed to be *noticing.*

Okay, Ben. Let's do the stupid exercise. Let's notice.

He closed his eyes for a second. And the wave hit him. It wasn't just a roommate. It was a stadium full of screaming, contradictory, terrified voices.

...she's mad at me. I'm a terrible husband...

...this is a waste of time, Johnson is probably emailing my client right now...

...I'm failing at this. I'm failing at relaxing. How can anyone fail at this?...

...my heart is racing. Am I having a heart attack? I'm too young for a...

"Thinking," he whispered, trying to hold on to Maya's two-word lifeline.

He felt the tide of noise recede, just a little. He wasn't drowning in it. He was... on a rock, watching it surge around him. *Okay. I'm doing it. I'm noticing.*

"Thinking," he labeled a thought about work.

"Thinking," he labeled a thought about his health.

"Thinking," he labeled a thought about how stupid it was to be labeling his thoughts.

He felt a strange, fragile sense of calm. He was doing it. He was a good student. He would be the best at this. He would be the most mindful, most present person Maya had ever...

"Ben?"

He opened his eyes. Hannah was looking at him with a mixture of confusion and deep sadness.

"What?" he said, a little too sharply.

"I just... I asked if you'd at least be off your phone for Leo's birthday party tomorrow. And you just... you smiled. Like you were a million miles away."

Ben's stomach dropped. He hadn't heard a word. He had been so busy. So focused on *observing* his own mind, on *doing the practice right*, that he had been completely, utterly absent. He had just swapped one form of absence for another.

He had become an observer of his own thoughts, but he was still not a participant in his own life.

"Hannah, I..."

"It's fine," she said, the two most painful words in their marriage. She turned and walked out of the kitchen.

Ben stood alone. The silence in the room was louder than the stadium in his head. He had failed. He hadn't just been trapped by the roommate. He was trapped by the very effort to get free.

He wasn't just a man at war with his own mind. He was a man who wasn't even there.

He looked at his phone. He had to see Maya again. And this time, he wouldn't be bringing his Publicist. He'd be bringing a ghost.

Chapter - 4
The Ghost in the Room

Ben was at her door at 9:58 AM. He didn't sit in the waiting room. He stood, his arms crossed, a coiled spring of angry, desperate energy. When Maya opened the door at 10:00 on the dot, he walked past her.

"I'll have a coffee today," he said, sitting in the armchair.

"No, you won't," Maya said calmly, closing the door. She sat opposite him, her hands resting in her lap. "You look terrible, Ben. That's good. The Publicist is gone. Who showed up today?"

"A ghost," Ben said, the words coming out sharp. "Your technique is a failure. It made it worse."

He explained what happened with Hannah. He didn't spare himself. He described the scene in the kitchen, the grotesque irony of being so busy *noticing* his thoughts that he became a blank, smiling wall to his wife.

"I wasn't there," he finished, his voice raw. "I was a million miles away, patting myself on the back for being 'mindful.' She looked at me like I was a stranger. I *am* a stranger. What's your fix for that, huh?"

Maya was quiet for a long time. She didn't look disappointed. She looked... interested.

"You're right," she said. "It is a failure. A necessary one. A very, very good failure."

"How is that *good*?" Ben snapped.

"Because you were still trying to win. You, Ben, are a world-champion achiever. You turned the simple act of *noticing* into a new, high-stakes project. A project you could 'be the best at.' You were in your head, on a balcony, watching a play about your life. You were taking notes, grading your own performance. But you were still not *in* the play."

She leaned in, and her simple, direct gaze felt like an anchor.

"You're not a ghost because you have a busy mind, Ben. You're a ghost because you live in two places, neither of which are real."

"What are you talking about?"

"**Yesterday and Tomorrow**," she said. "You haunt your own life. When you were in that kitchen with Hannah, your mind wasn't in the kitchen. It was on Monday's proposal. That's **Tomorrow**. A place that doesn't exist. Then, when she spoke to you, your mind instantly jumped to the argument you'd had, or the guilt you felt. That's **Yesterday**. A place that is dead and gone."

"No one can live in two different fantasies at the same time and also be present for their real life. It's impossible. The 'roommate' you hate so much? His only fuel is Yesterday and Tomorrow. He starves in the **Now**."

"So 'labeling' him was the wrong tool," Ben said, feeling a new wave of frustration.

"It was the first tool," Maya corrected. "It showed you that you are not your thoughts. Now, you need the second tool. You need to learn how to get off the balcony and onto the stage. You need to learn how to come home to the *only* moment you will ever have, which is this one."

"Right. Be present. I've read a hundred articles on that. It's meaningless."

"It's meaningless because it's an idea," she said. "Let's make it real. Close your eyes."

Ben sighed but did it. "Okay. They're closed."

"I want you to feel the fabric of your trousers on your legs. Just... feel the texture. Is it rough? Smooth?"

Ben's mind immediately said, This is stupid. This is the most expensive therapy in London and I'm feeling my pants.

"Thinking," Maya said, as if she could hear his thoughts. "Don't label it. Just let it go. Come back to the fabric. Just for one second."

Ben tried. He focused. It's... wool. A bit scratchy.

"Good," she said. "Now, feel your feet on the floor. Wiggle your toes inside your shoes. Feel the solid ground beneath you. It's holding you up. You are, in this exact second, right here."

Ben did. He felt the sole of his shoe, the slight pressure in his left heel.

"Now open your eyes," she said.

He did. The room looked... sharper. The green of the plant in the corner seemed more vibrant. The "roommate" was, for a split second, completely silent. Not because Ben was fighting him. But because Ben had simply been somewhere else. He had been in his feet.

"That's the anchor," Maya said. "Your mind is a frantic, windswept kite. 'Labeling' is realizing you're holding the string. But the **anchor** is what keeps you from being blown away."

"That's it?" Ben asked, almost insulted. "Feel my feet?"

"That's it," she smiled. "Your brilliant, high-speed, partner-level brain is going to hate how simple this is. It's going to tell you it's stupid. But that's the practice. Your mind is in the past, feeling guilt about Hannah? Come back. Feel your feet on the floor. Your mind is in the future, panicking about the Johnson account? Come back. Feel the teacup in your hand. Feel the air on your skin."

She stood up, signaling the end of the session.

"Your assignment, Ben, is not to 'think' about being present. Your assignment is to **physically arrive**. When you are in a meeting, feel your chair. When you are talking to your son, feel his hand in yours. Stop trying to silence the roommate and just start showing up in the room with him. He hates being ignored."

Chapter - 5
The Anchor in the Storm

Monday morning. The 41st floor. The big conference room.

It was the scene of the crime.

Ben was walking into the follow-up meeting about the Johnson account, the very account he had been catastrophizing over. And, as if the universe had a cruel sense of humor, Johnson himself was being patched in via video from New York.

The "roommate" was not just screaming; he was holding a rock concert.

...he's going to try and humiliate you. He's going to steal this. Sarah is watching. This is it. This is where they find you out...

Ben's heart was a hummingbird in his chest. His palms were damp. He took his seat. He was a ghost again, a vibrating, terrified ghost. Sarah opened the meeting.

"Ben, Mark," she said, nodding to him and to the large screen where Mark Johnson's perfectly coiffed, smiling face resided. "We all know there's been some friction on this proposal. Mark, you've raised some significant concerns. Ben, you're the lead. I want this solved, now."

This was it. The ambush.

"Thanks, Sarah," Johnson said, his voice smooth as oil. "Ben, look, I just want what's best for the client. And frankly, the risk exposure in your team's current model is... well, it's just not up to par. It's reckless. I've drafted an alternative..."

The room went silent. It was a direct, professional assassination attempt.

Ben felt the familiar, hot white flash of anger. His "Publicist" and "Roommate" grabbed the controls.

...Reckless? How dare he. He's a glorified salesman. I'll destroy him. I'll list his three biggest failures from the last quarter...

...He's right. You failed. You are reckless. You're a fraud...

The two voices were shouting at the same time, a dizzying, paralyzing vortex of Yesterday and Tomorrow. He was gone. Lost.

He opened his mouth to snap, to defend, to justify.

And then, a thought. Not a shout, but a whisper.

Maya. Come back. Feel your feet.

It was the stupidest, most simple idea in the world. But he was drowning. He would grab anything.

He pressed his feet into the plush, aggressively corporate carpet of the conference room. He felt the fibers, the solid concrete floor beneath them.

He felt the cold, smooth wood of the conference table under his palms. He focused on the grain of the wood, the way the light hit it.

He took one single, silent, unnoticeable breath.

The miracle was not that the anger vanished. It didn't.

The miracle was not that the fear vanished. It didn't.

The miracle was that *he was still there*.

He could feel the anger, a hot ball in his chest. He could feel the adrenaline, a cold zing in his veins. But he could *also* feel his feet on the floor. He could *also* feel the wood of the table.

For the first time in his life, he was not *lost* in the storm. He was the anchor, and the storm was just... weather.

He was in the room.

He looked at Johnson on the screen. And because he was *present*, he saw something new. He didn't just see a rival. He saw the slight, nervous flicker in Johnson's eyes. The way his smile didn't quite reach them. He saw a man who was also performing, a man who was also driven by his own roommate, his own fear.

The silence had stretched. It was Ben's turn.

He didn't attack. He didn't defend. He unlaced his fingers, placed his hands calmly on the table, and nodded.

"Thank you, Mark," Ben said. His voice was quiet. It was his own.

The entire room, including Johnson on the screen, looked surprised. They had all expected a fight.

"You're right," Ben continued. "You've pointed out the exact three risks that my team and I have been focused on. The currency fluctuation, the regulatory risk in the new market... they are significant."

Sarah's eyebrows shot up. This was not the normal Ben. The old Ben would be in a red-faced debate.

"What I think you're missing, Mark," Ben said, not as an attack, but as a statement of fact, "is the mitigation strategy we've built in. If you'll look at page 14 of the proposal..."

He was calm. He was clear. He wasn't a hero. He wasn't a genius. He was just... a man in a room, doing his job. He wasn't fighting his own mind. He was just present.

The meeting ended twenty minutes later. The Johnson "ambush" had fizzled into a productive discussion. Sarah gave Ben a long, appraising look as they packed up. It was a look of new respect.

Ben walked back to his office. He didn't feel euphoric. He didn't feel "zen." He just felt... solid.

He sat down. His roommate was still there, but his voice was quieter. He was muttering in the corner now, not screaming in Ben's face.

Ben Harris, for the first time in a long time, was home.

Chapter - 6
The Man Who Became a Cloud

Ben was a good student. He was, as Maya had pointed out, a world-champion achiever. And for the next two weeks, he achieved the hell out of mindfulness.

He became a master of the anchor.

When his inbox flooded, he felt his feet on the floor. When a junior associate fumbled a presentation, he felt the cool wood of the table. When his "roommate" screamed about a future deadline, he would simply label it "Thinking," take a breath, and come back to the solid ground of his own body.

He had found a superpower. He had found a secret, soundproof booth in the middle of the chaos.

The problem was, he had started to live in it.

He was in a review with Tom, a young, brilliant, and visibly panicked associate. Tom's numbers were off. He was stammering, trying to explain a data-entry error.

"...and I just, I don't know how I missed it, Ben, I was working on the other file, and my kid was sick, and..."

The Old Ben would have torn him to shreds. "Excuses are not a strategy, Tom."

The New Ben, the Mindful Ben, was different. He was anchored. He wasn't angry. He was... nothing. He watched Tom's panic as if it were a weather pattern on a screen. He observed his own fleeting impulse to be annoyed, labeled it "Thinking," and let it drift by. He was a perfect, calm, blue sky.

"Tom," Ben said, his voice so profoundly calm it was almost eerie. "I'm observing a great deal of agitation in you."

Tom's stammering stopped. "Uh... what?"

"You're lost in a story about Yesterday," Ben said, genuinely trying to be helpful. "The mistake is made. You're not in the Now. You need to come back to the anchor. Just feel your feet on the floor."

Tom looked at Ben's feet, then at his own, then back at Ben. The young man's panic was instantly replaced by a new, more profound emotion: total, bewildered confusion.

"Sir... I... the numbers..."

"The numbers are just numbers," Ben said, with the gentle confidence of a man who has just discovered the secrets of the universe. "We will fix them. But you can't fix them until you are present."

Tom left the office ten minutes later, more terrified than when he had entered. He hadn't just made a mistake; he had been given a bizarre zen riddle by a boss who had apparently joined a cult.

Ben, meanwhile, felt a small, satisfied puff of pride. He had handled that with real presence. He was getting good at this. His roommate was now his biggest fan. *Look at you, Ben. So calm. So evolved. Tom was a mess. You've really got this under control.*

He brought this new, enlightened energy home.

That night, Hannah was talking. She was animated, her hands moving as she described a conflict she was having with her sister.

"...and she just said, right in front of Mom, that I was the one who always..."

Ben was listening. He was being a *fantastic* listener. He was fully present. He wasn't thinking about work. He was observing her. He was noticing her "agitation." He was seeing her "roommate" screaming. He was anchored.

"...so what do you think I should do?" she finally asked, looking to him for connection, for support.

Ben took a calming breath, just as Maya had taught him. "Well," he said, in his new, gentle, measured tone, "it sounds like you're letting her story hook you. Your frustration is just a result of your own unmet expectations. If you were just present with the situation, her words wouldn't have any power over you."

Hannah's face, which had been open and pleading, went perfectly, dangerously still.

"What?" she said.

"It's just her 'roommate' talking," Ben explained, warming to his topic. "It's not the real her. Just like your anger isn't the real you. It's just 'Thinking.' If you just..."

"Stop."

Her voice was ice.

"Stop... what?" Ben asked, genuinely confused.

"Stop... *this*. This... calm, floaty,... whatever this is. You're not here."

"Hannah, that's absurd. I'm more here than I've ever been! I'm not on my phone, I'm not thinking about work, I'm..."

"No," she said, and he saw her eyes were brimming with tears. "You're not. You're... you're *observing* me. Like I'm a... a project. A bug under a microscope. I don't want a guru, Ben. I want my husband."

She shook her head, a small, sad laugh escaping her. "You know, I think I miss the old Ben. At least when he was an anxious, work-obsessed jerk, he was *in the mud* with me. At least he was *real*."

She turned and walked into the bedroom, closing the door behind her. Not slamming it. A quiet, final click.

Ben stood in the living room, alone. The silence was deafening.

His anchor was gone. He couldn't feel his feet. He couldn't feel the floor. He had used his new tools to build a brand new, even more perfect, even more lonely glass office around himself.

He wasn't a ghost anymore. He was a cloud. A calm, present, useless cloud, floating six inches above the world, unable to touch or be touched by anything real.

He pulled out his phone. He had to see Maya.

Chapter - 7
The Umbrella in the Rain

The dark green door felt heavier this time. He didn't knock. He just pushed it open and walked in, dripping rain from his overcoat onto the simple rug.

Maya was there, as if she was expecting him. She didn't have tea ready. She just looked at him, her hands in the pockets of her cardigan.

"You look like a man who just lost a fight with a cloud," she said.

"I am the cloud," Ben said. His voice was flat. "A calm, present, useless cloud."

He didn't wait to be invited. He sank into the armchair, the fight completely gone out of him. He told her everything. He told her about Tom, the associate, and the look of baffled terror in his eyes. And he told her about Hannah. He told her the line that had been echoing in his skull for twenty-four hours: *"I think I miss the old Ben. At least when he was... a jerk, he was in the mud with me."*

"She's right," Ben finished, looking at his hands. "I'm not in the mud. I'm floating. And it's so... lonely, Maya. It's the loneliest I've ever been. I've become a... a benign, smiling sociopath."

Maya let the silence sit. It was not an empty silence. It was a warm silence, like a blanket.

"Good," she said, finally.

"Good? I just told you I've ruined my marriage by being a 'calm, floaty' whatever. How is that good?"

"Because you've found the limits of the tool," she said, finally sitting down opposite him. "You, Ben, are a high-performance machine. You took the tools I gave you—labeling, anchoring—and you achieved a perfect 100 on the test. You successfully... *observed*."

She leaned forward. "But life is not a laboratory, Ben. It's a dance. And you were using a microscope when you were supposed to be listening to the music."

"What does that mean?"

"You learned to be the sky to your *own* storm. A brilliant, necessary, and life-changing first step. But then you turned that same gaze on others. You observed Tom's panic as 'weather.' You observed Hannah's pain as 'her story.' You stayed in your perfect, calm, safe, blue sky, while they were on the ground, drowning. And from your great height, you yelled down... 'Have you tried not being wet?'"

Ben flinched. The metaphor was perfect. It was exactly what he had done.

"You're right," he whispered. "So what's the answer? Do I just... go back to being a jerk in the mud?"

"No," Maya said, her voice full of warmth. "You don't have to be buried in the mud to be in it. You've learned how to find your anchor. You've learned how to not get swept away. You don't have to be the storm. But you're not meant to be the cloud, either."

"Then what am I?"

"You're the lighthouse," she said. "The anchor. You're the one who is solid. You're supposed to be a place of safety for other people's storms. You're not supposed to *judge* their storm, or *fix* their storm. You're just supposed to be *with* them in it."

She smiled. "You used the anchor to save yourself. And then you pulled it up and floated away. You were never meant to float. You were meant to become an anchor for *other people*."

Ben was quiet. "When Hannah was... in her storm... what was I supposed to do? Tell me what to do."

"Ah, 'tell me what to do,'" Maya said, tapping her chin. "The anthem of the achiever. The answer is so simple, your brilliant brain is going to reject it."

"Try me."

"Listen."

Ben waited. "Listen. That's it?"

"No, Ben. You've never done it. You *hear* people. You *assess* people. You *diagnose* people. You have not, perhaps in your entire adult life, simply *listened* to someone with no agenda other than to understand what it feels like to be them in that moment."

She continued. "When Hannah is in her pain, she doesn't need a calm guru to tell her her pain is an illusion. She needs her husband to see that she is in pain. That's it."

"So, what? I just nod and say 'uh-huh'?"

"No. You stop trying to *fix* her, and you just get curious. You ask questions. Not 'Why do you feel that way?' which is a judgment. But 'What's that like for you?' or 'Tell me more.' You're not there to solve her problem, Ben. You're there to make her feel that she is not alone *inside* her problem. You're not there to lecture her about the rain. You're there to bring an umbrella, sit down next to her, and just be with her in the storm until it passes."

It clicked. The "roommate," the "anchor," the "cloud"... they were all about *him*. His journey. His mind. His freedom. He had been on a solo expedition. But this... this was about other people.

"My 'zen' thing..." Ben said, the realization dawning, "...it was just another, more sophisticated, way for my ego to be in charge. The 'Enlightened Ben' was just as much a performance as the 'Successful Partner Ben.' It was just another, colder glass office."

Maya smiled. A real, brilliant smile. "And now you see it," she said. "Now you're ready to actually walk out the door."

Ben stood up. He felt... different. Not calm. Not enlightened. He just felt... human. And for the first time, that felt like enough.

"I need to go home," he said.

"Yes, you do," she said. "Your assignment, Ben, is to stop *observing* your life. Go get in the mud."

Chapter - 8
The Umbrella

He didn't go back to the office. He took a taxi straight home. It was 11:30 AM on a Saturday, a time he was usually on a spin bike, checking his email between sets.

He walked into his own home like a guest. It was quiet. He could hear the faint sound of the TV in the playroom, where Leo was. He found Hannah in the living room, curled in the armchair by the window, a book open on her lap. She was just staring at the rain-streaked glass.

She looked up when he entered. He saw it, the flicker of a shield going up. Her body tensed, preparing for whichever version of him had walked in: the frantic, distracted Ben, or the new, disturbingly calm "Cloud Ben."

"You're home," she said. It wasn't a question. Her tone was flat, guarded.

The old Ben, the achiever, would have launched into his new thesis. *Hannah, I've had a profound realization! I've been a cloud! I've been observing you instead of connecting!* He would have presented his breakthrough as a finished project, another achievement.

His mouth opened. He could feel the Publicist itching to speak.

He stopped. He used his anchor. He felt his feet, not to float away, but to *stay*. To simply be in this tense, sad, real room with his wife.

He just stood there for a moment. He looked at her, really looked at her. He didn't *observe* her. He *saw* her. He saw the loneliness. He saw the exhaustion she had in her shoulders. He saw the woman who had been trying to hold a family together while her husband was at war with his own mind.

"Hi," he said, and his voice was rough.

"Hi," she replied, her eyes wary.

He didn't sit in the chair opposite her. That was a confrontation. He sat on the floor, leaning his back against the sofa, so he was near her, but not crowding her. He just sat, in silence, for a full ten seconds.

It was the longest, most present ten seconds they had shared in years.

"What you said last night," he finally said, his voice quiet. He didn't look at her. He looked at the rain. "You were right. I miss the old Ben, too."

He heard her shift in the chair. He felt her surprise.

"I... I didn't mean..."

"No," he said, turning to look at her. "You did. And you were right. That... that jerk, the one who was in the mud? At least he was real. At least he was *here*."

He let out a short, painful breath that was almost a laugh. "This 'calm' me... this... cloud. It's just another performance, Hannah. Just another, colder, glass office. I was using it to hide. To float above everything. To not... feel. And in the process, I made you feel..."

"Alone," she finished for him. Her voice was just a whisper.

"Yeah."

He looked at her, and his only agenda was to understand. "What's it been like?" he asked. "Being married to me, this last year? This... this ghost."

Hannah looked down at her book, her fingers tracing the cover. He could see her wrestling with a lifetime of his impatience, his defensiveness, his habit of fixing. She was deciding if it was safe.

Ben just waited. He held the silence. He didn't fill it with his own agenda. He didn't prompt her. He just held the umbrella, and waited.

And then, a tear rolled down her cheek and landed on the page.

"It's been... so... *lonely*," she whispered. "It's like I'm a window you just look through, on your way to the next problem. Or I'm a project you're trying to solve. You... you *diagnose* me, Ben. You don't *hold* me."

She looked at him, her face a mess of love and pain. "I don't need you to be a guru. I don't need you to be calm and enlightened. I just need you to be here. I need my partner back."

The old Ben would have had a ten-point plan.

1. Schedule date night.
2. Buy flowers.
3. Meditate less.

The new Ben did something he hadn't done in a long time. He felt. He didn't observe his own sadness. He just... felt sad. He felt the weight of the pain he had caused. He was in the mud with her.

He didn't move. He didn't try to fix her. He just nodded, his own eyes burning.

"Okay," he said.

"Okay? That's it?"

"Yeah," he said, his voice thick. "Okay. I'm here. I'm not... I'm not going to float away again. I'm here."

He reached out, not to grab her, but just an open hand on the floor between them. An invitation.

She looked at his hand for a long time. Then, slowly, she reached down from the chair and put her hand in his. It was the first real contact they had made in months. It wasn't a fix. It wasn't a solution. It was just... an anchor.

And for the first time, it wasn't just holding him. It was holding both of them.

Chapter - 9
The Mud

The next two weeks were not a miracle. They were a series of small, clumsy, difficult negotiations with reality.

There were moments Ben reverted, where the "roommate" grabbed the microphone and he snapped at Hannah about something trivial. There were times he "floated" again, catching himself observing his son Leo's laughter instead of just... laughing with him.

But the difference was, he *saw* it. And he'd apologize. "Sorry," he'd say to Hannah, "the jerk is back. My bad." And she would give him a small, real smile. The repair was faster. The connection was stronger.

The real test, he knew, was not at home. It was on the 41st floor.

It came on a Thursday afternoon.

A frantic knock on his open office door. It was Tom, the young associate. He didn't just look panicked. He looked like he had seen a ghost. He was pale, and his hands were visibly shaking.

Ben's first, automatic thought was, Oh God, what now? This is going to ruin my afternoon. The old, cold impatience.

His second thought was, I am observing his agitation. He is lost in a story. The new, floaty cloud.

He took a breath. He felt his feet on the floor, not to detach, but to stay. He looked at the young man, not as a problem, but as a person.

Maya's voice. Bring an umbrella.

"Tom," Ben said, his voice calm and, for the first time, genuinely warm. "Come in. Sit down. You look like you're about to fall over. What's going on?"

Tom sat, but more like a puppet whose strings had been cut. He just stared at his trembling hands, laced together so tightly his knuckles were white.

"I... I missed it," Tom whispered.

"Missed what?" Ben asked gently.

"The filing. The 4PM deadline. For the merger. I... I had the wrong date in my calendar. I had it for tomorrow. I just saw the email... the final, final, 4PM email..."

The "roommate" in Ben's head didn't just start to talk. He detonated.

THIS IS A CATASTROPHE. A multi-million-pound deal. You will be RUINED. This is HIS fault. END HIM.

Ben could feel the adrenaline. It was a physical, burning-hot spike, surging up his spine. His entire career, his reputation. He could feel the words forming in his mouth, the ones that would sever an artery: *How could you be so STUPID?*

He felt his feet on the floor. He gripped the edge of his own desk, his anchor in a 10-megaton storm.

He was here. This was real.

He looked at Tom. The kid looked like he was about to be physically sick. He was just a kid. He was a 28-year-old Ben, terrified of his own shadow.

Ben took a long, slow, agonizing breath. He was in the mud.

"Okay," Ben said. His voice was tight, but it was steady. "Okay. That... is a very big problem."

Tom flinched, bracing for the explosion.

Ben just nodded. He didn't fix. He didn't yell. He just... sat with him in the awful, awful truth.

"What's it like, for you, right now?" Ben asked, the words feeling foreign in his mouth.

Tom looked up, his eyes wide with disbelief.

"What?"

"What's it like?" Ben repeated. "In your head. Right now."

Tom stared at him. And then, something in the young man's face just... broke.

"It's... I can't breathe," Tom whispered, tears welling. "It's not just this. It's everything. I'm working 90 hours a week. I haven't seen my wife. I don't know my son. I'm drowning, Ben. I am... I'm so tired. I feel like a fraud every single day. And now... now this. I... I think I just ended my career."

Ben sat. He listened. He heard his own story. He heard the ghost he used to be. The panic, the pressure, the loneliness.

He let the silence sit for a full minute. His own "roommate" was still shouting, CALL LEGAL! CALL SARAH! FIX IT!

He would. In a minute. Not now.

"No, you didn't," Ben said, his voice firm, but not unkind.

Tom looked up.

"You didn't end your career," Ben said. "You made a terrible, terrible mistake. But this isn't your mistake, Tom. It's mine."

"What?"

"You're on my team. Your burnout is my failure of leadership. Your isolation is my failure to connect. This... this is a team failure. And I'm the head of the team."

Ben stood up. He was anchored. He was clear.

"Okay," he said, and now his voice had a new energy. Not panic. But purpose. "Here's what we're going to do. We're not going to hide. We're not going to lie. We're going to own this."

He pointed to his own chair. "Sit here. You're going to call Sarah's assistant and get her on a video call. Now."

"Me? I... I can't..."

"Yes, you can. I'll be right next to you. And then, together, we are going to call the client."

"The client?" Tom looked like he was going to pass out.

"Yes. We are not going to send an email. We're going to get on a call, we are going to tell them exactly what happened, and we are going to tell them exactly what we are going to do to fix it. This is not your call to make, Tom. It's our call."

Tom was trembling. But he nodded.

"Tom," Ben said, stopping him for one second. "This is the mud. It's awful. But the only way out is through. And you're not in it alone. Now, make the call."

Ben stood next to the desk, his hand on the young associate's shoulder, and for the first time in his entire career, he wasn't a partner, or a boss, or a guru, or a cloud. He was just... an umbrella. And he was ready for the rain.

Chapter - 10
The Call

Tom's hand was shaking so badly he could barely type Sarah's name into the video client. Ben placed his own hand on the desk, palm up, an open, steady anchor. He didn't say anything. Tom took a shuddering breath, looked at Ben's hand, and then, with a sharp, jabbing finger, clicked the "Call" button.

The screen lit up. Sarah's face appeared. She was in a different conference room, one with a view of the evening skyline. She was not smiling.

"Ben. Tom. This is a surprise. I'm in the middle of a board dinner. This had better be the building on fire."

The "roommate" in Ben's head screamed. *Abort! Abort! She's with the board! This is the worst possible time! This is your career ending in real-time!*

Ben felt his feet on the floor. He was anchored. He was here. He would not let Tom do this alone.

"Sarah," Ben said, his voice level. It cut through the static in his own head. "Thank you for picking up. This is a Code Red. I have to inform you that we have made a significant failure on the merger filing. We've missed the 4PM deadline."

Sarah's face didn't move. She didn't blink. The professional, high-stakes mask was perfect. But Ben, now a student of human weather, saw the pupils dilate. He saw the micro-second of pure, cold shock.

"Say that again," she said, her voice dropping ten degrees.

"A critical filing deadline for the merger was 4PM today," Ben said, clearly and without excuses. "It was not filed. The error was on my team. Tom here is the one who discovered the mistake and, with full integrity, brought it to me immediately. I've asked him to be on this call."

He had done it. He had taken the bullet for the team ("my team"), given Tom credit for the integrity, and shared the "mud" with him ("I've asked him to be on this call").

Sarah's gaze shifted to Tom. It was the gaze of a hawk. "Explain."

Tom looked at Ben. Ben gave a single, almost imperceptible nod. *You can do this. You are not alone.*

Tom sat up. His voice shook, but it didn't break. "Sarah, this was my error. One hundred percent. I had the deadline marked for tomorrow. I don't know why. I just... I had the wrong date. I was checking the file to prepare for tomorrow, and I saw the 4PM timestamp. I missed it. It's on me."

There it was. The truth. No excuses. No "my kid was sick." No "90-hour week." Just the raw, awful fact.

Sarah closed her eyes for exactly two seconds. Ben knew what she was doing. She was calculating. She was running the numbers. The potential lawsuits. The client implosion. The market implications.

When she opened her eyes, the shock was gone. Only fire remained.

"Do you two have any idea what you've just done?" she hissed. "Do you? The client... the board... this isn't a mistake, Tom. This is an immolation. You haven't just missed a deadline; you've potentially scuttled a 500-million-pound deal."

Tom withered. He physically shrank in the chair.

And this was the moment. The old Ben would have joined in. *Yes, Tom, how could you!* He would have sacrificed his associate to save his own skin.

Ben leaned forward into the camera, placing himself between Sarah and Tom.

"Yes, Sarah," Ben said, his voice still quiet, still firm. "We understand the gravity. And as I told Tom, this is not his failure. This is my failure."

Sarah was stunned into silence.

"That error," Ben continued, "is a symptom. The symptom is a culture of burnout, of 90-hour weeks, and of a team that is running so hot they are making simple, catastrophic mistakes. That is not Tom's fault. That is my fault, as his manager. I have been leading my team straight into the ground."

It was the most terrifyingly honest thing he had ever said in his professional life. He had just handed Sarah his own head on a platter.

Sarah just stared. She was speechless. She had a playbook for angry, defensive, blame-shifting employees. She had no playbook for this.

"Ben..." she said, her voice losing its edge, now just confused.

"I will be submitting a full post-mortem on my own management failures," Ben said. "But that is for tomorrow. For *right now*, we have one priority. It's the client. The client is still in their New York office. We have to call them. Now."

Sarah's eyes widened. "Call them? Are you insane? We call legal. We draft a statement. We..."

"No," Ben said. "We do not hide. Hiding is what got us here. We are going to call them, leader to leader. We are going to tell them the unvarnished truth, we are going to apologize, and we are going to present our solution for an immediate emergency refiling, which I have already drafted."

He held up a single piece of paper. He had been preparing it while Tom was making the call.

There was a long, electric silence. Sarah looked at Ben, then at Tom, then back to Ben. She was seeing a man she had never seen before. The man she had hired was a brilliant, anxious, selfish performer. This man was... a leader.

"My God," she whispered, rubbing her temple. "Okay, Ben. Okay. You're right. You and Tom make the call. But you loop in legal's line *immediately*. I'll text you their home number. I'll start managing the board."

The screen went dark.

Ben and Tom sat in the silence. The "roommate" was nowhere to be found. There was no room for him. There was only the thumping of Ben's heart, a heavy drum in the quiet.

"Okay," Ben said, pulling his phone out. "One more call. You and me."

Tom nodded. He was still pale, still shaking. But his eyes were clear. He had just watched his boss detonate his own career to save his.

"Ben," Tom said, his voice hoarse.

"Yeah?"

"Whatever happens. Thank you."

Ben clapped him on the shoulder. "Don't thank me yet. We're still in the mud. Let's find the client's number."

Chapter - 11
The Confession

The office was dark. The only light came from the blue-white glow of the monitor and the sprawling, indifferent city lights beyond the glass. It was 9 PM. On Ben's speakerphone, three lines were open.

Line 1: Davies, the firm's general counsel, patched in from his living room. He was audibly, professionally, terrified.

Line 2: Tom, sitting across from Ben, pale as a sheet, but present.

Line 3: The line for the client. It was ringing.

"Ben, let me do the talking," Davies said, his voice a tight whisper. "This is a procedural notification. We state the facts, we reference section 4.B of the agreement, we do not, under any circumstances, admit liability..."

"No, Davies," Ben said quietly, his hand on the desk, feeling the wood. "We do not."

"Ben, I am advising you as..."

"Mr. Harris?" A new voice, sharp, crackling with transatlantic authority, filled the room. "You have sixty seconds. I am in a car. This is Kael."

Mr. Kael. The client. The one who never spoke. The one whose *people* had people.

"Davies, mute," Ben commanded. He hit the mute button on Davies's line.

"Ben, don't you..." Davies's voice was cut off.

Ben looked at Tom. He nodded. He was in the mud. He was holding the umbrella. He unmuted their line.

"Mr. Kael. This is Ben Harris. Thank you for taking the call."

"I'm not taking the call, Harris. I'm on it. You have fifty seconds."

Ben's roommate screamed. *This is it. This is the end. Lie. Spin it. Blame the system. Blame the deadline.*

"Mr. Kael," Ben said, and his voice was so calm, it surprised him. "We have made a catastrophic error. A 4PM filing deadline for the merger was missed today by my team."

There was no sound from the speaker. Just the faint, empty hiss of an open international line. Ben could hear his own blood pounding in his ears.

"A... what?" Kael's voice was no longer sharp. It was a cold, flat, dangerous thing.

"We missed the filing," Ben said. "The error was ours. One hundred percent. We failed you."

He could hear Davies trying to break in, probably smashing his mute button.

"Do you know what I do, Harris?" Kael said, his voice a soft, venomous drawl. "I build things. I build factories. I build them in countries where the concrete is bad and the government is worse. It's a business built on one thing. Trust. It's built on knowing that when a man says 'the bolt is tightened,' the bolt is... *tightened.*"

"Yes, sir."

"And you... you, with your 800-dollar-an-hour fee... you just told me you didn't tighten the bolt."

"That is correct, sir. And as the head of this team, that is my failure. Not just the bolt. The entire process. I am the one who failed you."

"Ben," Tom suddenly said, his voice small but clear.

Ben looked at him, surprised.

"Mr. Kael," Tom said, leaning in. "My name is Tom. I'm the associate who had the date wrong. I am the one who didn't tighten the bolt. What Mr. Harris is telling you is that he... he's the man who is rebuilding a culture here where people like me are too burned out to see the calendar straight. He's right. It's his failure. But I am the one who made the mistake. We are both on this line, sir, because we are not going to hide."

Another terrible, vast silence. Ben looked at Tom with a deep, profound sense of gratitude. He was not alone in the mud.

"So," Kael's voice finally said. "I am holding a 500-million-pound deal, and it is in the hands of a burned-out manager and a rookie who can't read a calendar. Is that the sum of it?"

"Yes, sir," Ben said. "And two men who will not lie to you. We have a draft for an emergency refiling. We've been on the phone with legal. We believe there is a path. It is a narrow one."

"I'm on a plane," Kael said. "I'm supposed to be flying to Hong Kong. I'm flying to London instead. I will land at Heathrow at 11:00 AM your time tomorrow."

He paused. Ben could hear the engine of Kael's car.

"You have until I land. You, Harris. You, Tom. You will be in my car. You will have a plan. Not a legal fix. A *viable* one. A real one. You will tell me how you are going to save my deal. And if you don't have one... don't bother showing up."

The line clicked. He was gone.

Ben and Tom sat in the darkness. The only sound was the faint, frantic "Ben! BEN!" from Davies's muted line.

Ben calmly unmuted it.

"Yes, Davies? We're here."

"HAVE YOU LOST YOUR MIND? ADMITTING LIABILITY! 'FAILURE'! 'BURNED OUT'! YOU..."

"Davies," Ben cut him off. "We have a new deadline. 11:00 AM tomorrow. At Heathrow. Are you going to help us, or are you going to shout?"

Davies was silent for a beat. He was a lawyer, but he was also a shark. And he smelled a new kind of power.

"...Heathrow?" Davies said, his voice shifting from panic to calculation. "Okay. Okay. I'll be in your office in thirty minutes. We're going to need more coffee."

Ben hung up. He looked at Tom. The kid was exhausted, but he was alive. His career hadn't ended. It had just begun.

"Go home, Tom," Ben said.

"What? Sir, I'm staying. I'll..."

"No. You're not. You're going to go home. You're going to kiss your wife. You're going to hug your son. You're going to get six hours of sleep. I need you anchored and clear tomorrow, not burned out. That's an order. I'll be here with Davies. Be here at 7 AM."

Tom just nodded, his eyes wide. He stood up, walked to the door, and paused.

"7 AM, Ben," he said. He didn't call him "sir."

"7 AM, Tom," Ben replied.

Ben was alone in the glass office. It was no longer a prison. It was a command center. He had 14 hours. He felt his feet on the floor, rolled up his sleeves, and turned on the lights. The roommate was silent. There was work to do.

Chapter - 12
The Longest Night

By 10 PM, the 41st floor was a battlefield of paper cups and discarded legal pads. Davies, his tie pulled loose, was pacing in front of the whiteboard, which was covered in frantic legal scrawls.

"It's a black-letter violation, Ben, there's no way around it," Davies said, his voice raw from coffee. "We're dead. Our best bet is to file for a procedural stay, cite a 'system-wide server error'—we can get IT to backdate a log..."

"No."

Davies stopped pacing. "No? What do you mean, 'no'? I'm trying to give us cover! Spin!"

"We're not spinning," Ben said. He was sitting at the conference table, not pacing, just... still. He was looking out the window at the dark, silent city. "Kael didn't ask for cover. He asked for a plan. A *viable* one."

"A viable plan for what? Undoing yesterday? We don't have a time machine, Ben!"

"No," Ben said, turning back to the room. He was anchored. "We don't. So what's the real problem? The filing is a symptom. What's the disease?"

Davies looked at him, baffled. "The disease is a 500-million-pound deal going up in smoke! The disease is the client suing us into oblivion! The disease is..."

"The disease is trust," Ben said. "Kael said it himself. He doesn't trust us. But more than that, what's Kael's *real* fear? He's not afraid of us. He's afraid of the sellers. He's afraid the other side will use this as an excuse to walk away or, worse, renegotiate."

A new energy entered the room. Davies's frantic, anxious pacing slowed. He was a shark, and Ben had just put blood in the water. Real, strategic blood.

"Go on," Davies said, picking up a pen.

"So, a legal fix is useless," Ben said, standing and moving to the whiteboard. He erased a section of Davies's "spin." "It doesn't rebuild trust. It doesn't solve Kael's *real* problem. We can't just fix the filing. We have to fix the deal."

For the next four hours, they didn't work as a lawyer and a partner. They worked as two minds focused on a single point. They gamed out the sellers' moves. They analyzed the personalities on the other side's board. They tore apart the contract, not looking for loopholes, but for levers of a different kind: levers of mutual interest, of shared risk, of personal pride.

They didn't find a legal argument. They found a strategy. It was a confession, but a confession wrapped in a solution. It was a plan that was as much about human psychology as it was about finance.

At 5:17 AM, they stopped. The plan was on the board. It was audacious. It was honest. And it was terrifying.

"This is the craziest damned thing I've ever seen," Davies said, slumping into a chair, utterly spent. "This isn't law. This is... I don't know what this is. But if he says 'yes,' it'll be a legend. If he says 'no,' you, me, and Tom are going to be a cautionary tale in a textbook."

"It's the only real move we have," Ben said. He felt exhausted, but he also felt... clean. He was in the mud, but he wasn't drowning.

The door to his office opened.

It was Tom. 7:00 AM on the dot. He was in a fresh suit, his hair was damp from a shower, and his eyes were clear. He was holding three cups of coffee.

"You're still here," Tom said. It wasn't a question. He handed a cup to Ben and one to Davies.

"We have a plan," Ben said.

Tom looked at the whiteboard. He read the three bullet points of their strategy. He was quiet for a long time.

"It's good," Tom said. "It's all about the 'why.' It's about Kael's trust."

Then he frowned. "But it's missing something."

Davies, who was about to inhale his coffee, stopped. "Missing? Kid, this plan is a Hail Mary made of... I don't know... pure integrity. What could it be missing?"

"The 'how,'" Tom said, turning to Ben. "The 'how' of us. We're telling Kael we have a new plan, but we're the same broken team. Why should he believe us? We're still the guys who are too burned out to read a calendar."

Ben looked at Tom. The kid wasn't just an associate. He was a leader. He had just found the hole.

"You're right," Ben said. "He's absolutely right. Kael's trust in the deal is one thing. His trust in us is another."

"So, what do we do?" Davies asked, now genuinely invested.

"We tell him the truth about that, too," Ben said. He grabbed a marker. "Step Four: The New Covenant."

For the next hour, the three of them—the partner, the lawyer, and the associate—didn't just plan how to save the deal. They outlined a new, public, and non-negotiable protocol for how their team would operate. Mandated rest periods. A "buddy" system for all critical filings. A "no-blame" post-mortem culture. They weren't just fixing a mistake. They were building a new machine.

At 9:30 AM, Ben grabbed his coat.

"It's 10:00 AM," Tom said, confused. "We have an hour."

"No, we don't," Ben said. "We're not going to meet him in his car. We're going to be standing on the curb when he pulls up. We're not going to be scrambling. We're going to be ready."

The three of them, a sleep-deprived and terrified team of architects, walked out of the glass office and into the elevator, holding a single-page plan that would either save everything, or be the last thing they ever did.

Chapter - 13
The Windsor Suite

The private terminal at Heathrow was a cathedral of quiet, gray efficiency. It was 10:15 AM. The air was cold, and the sky was the color of unpolished steel.

Ben, Tom, and Davies stood on the curb, not in the warmth of the lounge. They didn't speak. They just watched. Ben had made them get here an hour and a half early. Not to practice, but to anchor. To be so present, so rooted in the moment, that when the storm arrived, they would be the lighthouse, not the ship.

A black, impossibly sleek Maybach pulled up to the curb and stopped, its engine a low, predatory hum. The back door opened.

Mr. Kael emerged. He was not a large man, but he seemed to take up all the air on the tarmac. He was in a dark, perfectly tailored suit, no overcoat despite the cold. He looked at the three of them, his face unreadable, cold as the morning.

"You're here," he said. It sounded like an accusation. "Get in." He nodded toward the car.

Davies, the lawyer, instinctively took a step forward, his hand reaching for the door, ready to obey.

"No, sir."

The word, spoken by Ben, hung in the cold air. Davies froze. Tom held his breath.

Kael turned his full attention to Ben. His eyes were a flat, pale gray. He said nothing.

"Mr. Kael," Ben said, his voice quiet but carrying. He was anchored. He could feel the pavement through the soles of his shoes. "This is not a conversation for a car. This is a war room briefing. We've reserved the Windsor Suite for you, just inside. Coffee is hot. The plan is ready. We can begin when you are."

He held Kael's gaze. He did not plead. He did not posture. He stated a fact.

Kael stared at him for a long, agonizing five seconds. He was a man who lived his life in cars, on planes, in motion. A man used to people jumping when he spoke. He was being asked to stop, to come to *them*.

The corner of Kael's mouth twitched. It was not a smile.

"You're costing me a lot of money, Ben Harris."

"I am aware of that, sir. Which is why I don't want to waste another minute of your time in a car."

Kael looked at Tom, who was holding a single, slim briefcase. He looked at Davies, who looked like he had just seen his own ghost. Finally, he looked back at Ben.

"Lead the way."

The Windsor Suite was a sterile, expensive room with a heavy mahogany table. A single document page was set at each of the four places.

Kael walked in, took the head of the table, but did not sit. "You have sixty seconds," he said, "to tell me why I shouldn't take this document, walk out that door, and spend the next five years of my life suing your firm into a fine, gray powder."

The "roommate" screamed in Ben's head. *He's angry! He's going to destroy us! Lie! Apologize! Grovel!*

Ben stood at his place. He felt his feet.

"Because the men who failed you are not in this room," Ben said.

Kael's eyebrows shot up. "Oh? Then who, exactly, are you?"

"You're looking at the men who are going to save your deal," Ben said. "We're not here to give you a legal excuse, Mr. Kael. We are here to give you a win. And it starts with two problems. May I?" He motioned to the whiteboard.

Kael nodded. Just once.

"Problem one: our filing," Ben said, writing it on the board. "We missed it. It's a fact. It is a catastrophic failure of our process. Problem two..." He wrote on the board, larger. "The *real* problem. The sellers. The other side now has a legal, moral, and financial window to either walk away or, worse, bleed you dry in renegotiations."

He turned. He had Kael's full, undivided attention.

"Our plan," Ben said, "is not about fixing problem one. The legal fix is just paperwork. Our plan is about solving problem two."

He laid out the audacious, three-point strategy they had built during the night. It wasn't about legal filings. It was about leveraging the sellers' other market risks, about back-channeling to a key board member, about presenting a new, *better* closing offer that was actually a concession in their favor. It was a masterpiece of psychology, disguised as a legal strategy.

Davies, to his credit, stepped in and laid out the legal mechanics of it with flawless precision. He was a shark, and this was his water.

When they finished, Kael was silent.

"It's brilliant," he said, his voice flat. "And I don't trust a word of it."

Ben's heart sank.

"You're still the same team," Kael said. "You're still the burned-out manager and the rookie who can't read. This is a beautiful plan. Why should I trust *you* to execute it? What happens next week, when your boy Tom here is too tired to send an email?"

This was it. The moment.

"That," Ben said, "is the most important part of the plan. Tom?"

Tom, who had been silent, stood up. He was no longer the trembling kid. He was a man who had walked through the fire and was still standing.

"Mr. Kael," Tom said, his voice clear. "You're right. Your trust in us is broken. Which is why we're not asking you to trust the old us. We're asking you to invest in a new one."

Tom walked to the whiteboard and, in the empty space, wrote: THE NEW COVENANT.

He laid out their fourth point. The new, non-negotiable protocols. The "buddy system" for all filings. The mandatory "dark" hours for the team to prevent burnout. The "blameless post-mortem" culture to catch mistakes early.

"This isn't just a promise, sir," Tom finished. "It's our new operating system. And it's public. We're asking for this to be an addendum to our contract with you. You'll have full transparency. We fail this, you fire us."

Kael looked at the board for a long, long time. He looked at Tom's covenant. He looked at Ben's audacious strategy.

He sat back. The silence in the room was absolute.

"You two..." Kael said, his voice a low rumble. "You are either the stupidest men I have ever met, or the most brilliant."

He paused, looking at Ben. "You called the sellers, didn't you?"

Ben's roommate screamed, Don't! Don't tell him!

Ben felt his anchor. "No, sir. I couldn't call them without your authority. But I did call their head of legal. An old contact."

"And?" Kael said, leaning forward.

"And I told him I needed to speak to him and his client at 11:30 this morning, with you, about a time-sensitive, mission-critical revision to the deal. He's on standby, Mr. Kael."

A slow, dangerous smile spread across Kael's face. It was the first time Ben had ever seen him smile. It was terrifying.

"You're a damned pirate, Harris."

"I'm your pirate, sir," Ben said.

Kael stood up. He buttoned his suit jacket.

"Okay, Ben. Okay. Get him on the phone. Get me my deal."

Chapter - 14
The Pirate's Gambit

The room was a pressurized cabin. The only sound was the faint click as Ben dialed the number on the conference phone. Kael was standing, not sitting, at the head of the table, a shark in his own element. Davies was shuffling papers, a nervous tic. Tom was perfectly still, his hands on his knees, breathing. Anchored.

The line picked up on the second ring.

"Reynolds." The voice was clipped, impatient, the sound of a man who bills in six-minute increments.

"Reynolds, this is Ben Harris," Ben said, his voice calm and clear. "I'm here with Mr. Kael."

A pause on the other end. Kael's name was a cannon shot.

"...Ben. I was expecting a call. Not, perhaps, with Mr. Kael on the line. What can I do for you?" Reynolds's voice was guarded, wary. He was smelling for a trap.

"I'm calling, as I mentioned, about a time-sensitive, mission-critical revision to the deal," Ben said.

"A revision?" Reynolds's voice sharpened. "Ben, the deal is signed. The terms are locked. We're in the quiet period. You know this."

"We do," Ben said. "And yet, a situation has developed. It's a two-part situation. The first part is procedural. The second is... strategic."

Kael, watching Ben, nodded almost imperceptibly. *Get to it.*

"The procedural part," Ben said, "is that we have had a full-scale failure on our side. A critical filing was missed yesterday. It's a material error, it is entirely our fault, and it creates a significant problem."

He didn't need to look at Davies to feel the lawyer's entire body clench.

On the phone, there was a sharp intake of breath, followed by a thick, triumphant silence. Reynolds was processing his sudden, spectacular good fortune.

"Missed?" Reynolds finally said, and Ben could hear the smile in his voice. "Ben, that's not just a 'problem.' That's a... that's a material breach. That's a fatal flaw. You know what that means. The deal is voidable. My clients... they're going to be... well, this changes everything."

"Yes," Ben said. "It does. It gives your side a choice. You can either take this mistake, blow up the deal, and we all spend the next three years in court. Or..."

"Or?" Reynolds said, savoring the word. "Or I can take this to my client and we can renegotiate the price. A *significant* price adjustment. You've handed us a golden-ticket, Ben."

"Or," Ben said, cutting him off, his voice dropping, "you can hear the strategic revision. The *second* part of the call."

"There is no second part, Ben. You've lost. Pay up."

"Here is the second part, Reynolds," Ben said, his voice like ice. "In light of this procedural failure, Mr. Kael no longer finds the original terms of the deal acceptable."

The silence that followed was so profound it felt like the phone line had been cut. Ben could feel Tom's eyes on him. He could feel Davies stop breathing. Kael... Kael was just watching, a statue of pure, predatory interest.

"What?" Reynolds's voice was a confused squawk. "You... *you* find the terms unacceptable? You're the ones who breached!"

"And this breach has forced us to re-evaluate the entire risk profile," Ben said, walking the tightrope. This was the pirate's gambit. "Our original agreement to absorb the regulatory risk in the new market... Mr. Kael is no longer comfortable with it. It's too high."

"You can't do that! You don't have the leverage!"

"We do," Ben said. "You have the breach. We have the capital. You can sue us. You'll win. In three years. It'll be a mess. Or, we can fix this. *Today*. Mr. Kael is prepared, in light of this... *new* situation... to increase his cash offer by three percent."

"Increase?" Reynolds was now utterly lost.

"Three percent," Ben confirmed. "In exchange for your client assuming the full regulatory risk in the new market."

It was the plan. The brilliant, insane plan. The new regulatory risk was exactly what the emergency refiling would be about. Ben was asking the other side to *take on the problem*, and he was offering to *pay them* to do it, all while disguised as a new, better offer. He was hiding the solution in plain sight.

"That's... you're offering *more* money... but you're asking us to take on the risk?" Reynolds was thinking, fast. "That's the part you never wanted to budge on."

"And you never wanted to budge on the price," Ben said. "It seems we've found a new, mutually beneficial path. This breach was a... a clarifying event. It showed us the weakness in the original deal. We are now proposing a stronger one. A cleaner one."

Kael spoke for the first time, his voice a low growl on the speakerphone. "Reynolds. This is Kael. My man is right. The original deal was weak. This one is strong. My new money, your new risk. That's the deal. It's a better deal for you. Do you want it or not?"

Reynolds was breathing heavily. He was a lawyer, not a principal. This was beyond his pay grade.

"I... I need to talk to my client. This is... I need to present this."

"You have one hour," Kael said. "We are refiling this entire, revised, stronger deal at 2 PM. We are holding a slot. We'd prefer your signature on the new terms. But we will be refiling regardless."

Kael looked at Ben.

"Right, Harris?"

Ben felt his feet on the floor. "2 PM is the deadline, Reynolds. One hour. Send us the signed addendum."

Ben hung up the phone.

The three of them stood in the room with Kael. The air was electric.

Tom let out a breath he seemed to have been holding since yesterday. Davies was looking at Ben with a kind of terrified awe.

Kael slowly sat down at the head of the table. He gestured for the coffee.

"Now," Kael said, as Ben poured him a cup. "We wait. And you, Harris..."

"Yes, sir?"

"You're going to tell me exactly what a 'blameless post-mortem' is."

Chapter - 15
The Engineer

There are two kinds of silence. There is the silence of the void, the heavy, anxious space where you wait for the axe to fall. And there is the silence of the forge, the hot, focused space after the hammer has struck, but before the metal has cooled.

The Windsor Suite was a forge.

Kael sat with his coffee, not drinking it, just holding it, letting the warmth seep into his hands. He was a man who built things, and he was watching three men attempt to build a new reality out of thin air.

"So," Kael said, his voice a low rumble. "This 'New Covenant.' This 'blameless post-mortem.' It sounds like you're giving your people a prize for failing. It sounds soft."

The "roommate" in Ben's head, high on the adrenaline of the last call, sprang to his feet. *Tell him how brilliant it is! Dazzle him with the philosophy! We are the new paradigm!*

Ben felt his feet on the floor. He let the wave of ego and adrenaline wash past him. He was not a guru. He was in the mud.

"No, sir," Ben said. "It's not soft. It's the opposite. It's brutally honest. It's a system for making it safe to find a mistake *early*, when it's small, instead of letting it fester in the dark until it's... well, until it's this."

Tom, who had been silent, leaned forward. He had earned his place at this table. "Mr. Kael, what I felt yesterday... what brought me to Ben's office... was terror. I was terrified of what would happen to *me*. I was ready to hide, to lie, to hope it went away. Because in our old system, a mistake wasn't just a fact. It was a... a moral failing. It meant *I* was a failure."

Ben picked up the thread. "A blameless post-mortem assumes everyone in the room is smart, capable, and was trying to do their best. So when a mistake happens, we don't ask, 'Who did this?' We ask, 'Why did our system allow this to happen?'"

"The wrench," Kael said, his eyes narrowing.

"Sir?"

"The bolt wasn't tightened," Kael said. "You're not asking *who* forgot to tighten it. You're asking *why* the wrench was broken. Or why the training was bad. Or why the man was on his 24th hour and couldn't see straight."

"Exactly," Ben said, a jolt of recognition passing between them. "We find the 'why' in the system. And then we share the findings with the *entire* team, so the lesson is only paid for once. We're not giving prizes for failure. We're making our failures productive."

Kael nodded slowly. "You're not a lawyer, Harris," he said, a strange look in his eye. "You're an engineer. A systems engineer. I understand systems."

The phone on the table rang. The display lit up: REYNOLDS.

The forge went silent. The hammer was about to fall.

Ben looked at Kael. Kael nodded. "Answer it. Speaker."

Ben pressed the button. The air in the room was so thick he could taste the ozone.

"Ben."

Reynolds's voice was not angry. It was not triumphant. It was the voice of a man who had just run a marathon in his mind. It was exhausted.

"You're a pirate, Harris. A goddamned pirate."

Ben felt his anchor. "Good afternoon, Reynolds. Do we have a deal?"

"My clients... they see the logic. They hate you. They hate me. But they see the logic. Your client's new cash offer is... solid. The risk... they'll take it. It's a clean break for them. It's... it's a good deal. A better one."

"So we have a signature?" Ben asked, keeping his voice perfectly level.

"The addendum is in your inbox. Signed. 2 PM. You hit your deadline," Reynolds said. There was a pause. "Don't ever, *ever* pull a stunt like this on me again."

"It wasn't a stunt, Reynolds. It was a clarification of a new reality."

The line clicked.

Davies let out a low whistle that was half-sob, half-gasp. Tom just closed his eyes, his head bowing, his shoulders shaking slightly with the release of a tension that had been building for twenty-four hours.

Ben stood. He was just... tired.

Kael finished his now-cold coffee in one gulp. He stood up. He buttoned his suit jacket. He looked at Ben.

"A systems engineer," he said again, as if to himself. He pulled a different card from his wallet. Not his corporate one. This one was thick, black, with only a name and a private number.

"I'm building a new foundation in Singapore," Kael said, sliding the card across the table. "I'm going to need a new architect. Someone who understands that the blueprints are only half the battle. Your 'New Covenant' is now an addendum to *my* contract. Don't... *ever*... make me use it."

"Yes, sir," Ben said.

"Good. Send me the bill. And Harris..." Kael paused at the door.

"Yes?"

"Your firm is going to bill me for every minute you three were in this room, on this call, and sweating in your office all night."

"Yes, sir. That's standard."

"I know," Kael said. "I want you to triple it. And I want the difference to go to this... this Tom. As a bonus. For finding the broken wrench."

He didn't wait for a reply. He just walked out.

Ben, Tom, and Davies were left alone in the room, with the silence and the smell of cold coffee. They had done it. They had walked through the fire and come out the other side. Ben looked at Tom, who was just staring at the black card on the table.

Ben smiled. A real, tired, human smile.

"Okay, Tom," he said, clapping him on the shoulder. "Let's go home."

Chapter - 16
The Day After

The adrenaline-fueled haze of the last 48 hours evaporated, leaving behind a profound, bone-deep exhaustion. The sun was streaming into the 41st-floor office. It was Friday. The rest of the firm was just... at work. Phones were ringing. Keyboards were clacking. Someone in the hallway was laughing about a weekend plan.

Ben and Tom had walked in at 10 AM, not as conquering heroes, but as two soldiers who had been the only ones to see the battle.

"It's... quiet," Tom said, standing by his cubicle.

"It's just an office," Ben replied, loosening his tie. He felt a strange dislocation. The world had almost ended, and the world hadn't even noticed.

He walked into his glass office. The whiteboard from the all-nighter was still there, a map of their impossible gambit. He looked at it, then erased the whole thing, every trace of Kael and Reynolds.

He took out a fresh marker. He had one more meeting to run.

At 4:00 PM, he called his team—all twelve of them—into the open-plan area by his office. Not the formal boardroom. He stood by a rolling whiteboard. The team shuffled in, looking anxious. A Friday 4 PM meeting with the head partner was never good news.

"Go ahead and grab a seat," Ben said. He waited until they were all settled.

He looked at their faces. Tired. Stressed. Each one of them a Tom-in-the-making, running too hot, too fast, too scared.

"As some of you know," Ben began, his voice quiet, "we had a near-miss this week. A failure. A procedural failure on my team."

He looked right at Tom. Tom met his gaze, steady.

"It was a mistake born of burnout. A mistake made possible because I have been leading this team as a machine, and a machine that is red-lined for too long, breaks. It was my failure of leadership. And it stops. Today."

He uncapped the marker and wrote on the whiteboard in big, clear letters:

THE NEW COVENANT.

He laid it out. Not as a complex legal addendum, but as their new constitution.

1. **THE BUDDY SYSTEM.** "Effective immediately, no critical filing, no final client proposal, ever leaves this office without two sets of eyes. One person

executes, a second, assigned buddy, signs off. No more heroes. We are a team."

2. **THE ANCHOR.** "We are not a machine. I am mandating a 'dark' period. No emails, no replies, from anyone on this team between 8 PM and 7 AM on weekdays. And I mean it. Not a single one. And Saturdays are your own. If I see you online, I will send you home. Your families deserve you. Your brain deserves you."

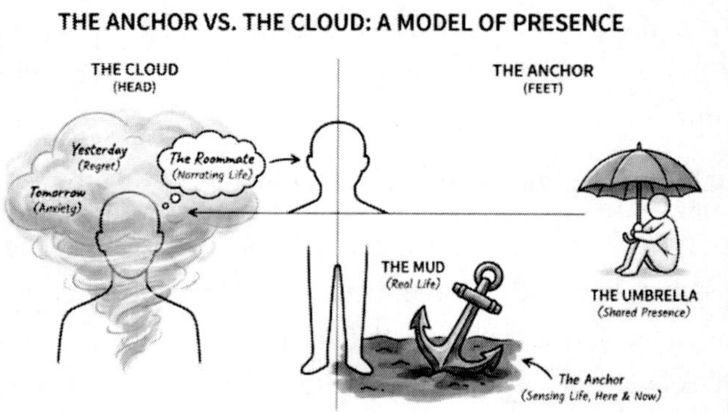

Figure 1: The Cycle of Presence

The Trap (The Glass Office): When we are lost in the "Cloud" of our thoughts, we are trapped by The Roommate. We live in the regrets of Yesterday or the fears of Tomorrow. In this state, we are merely observers of our life—visible, but disconnected.

The Solution (The Mud): To escape, we use The Anchor (feeling the feet on the floor) to bring our attention down out of the head and into the body. This grounds us in the Here and Now. Once anchored, we can open The Umbrella, shifting from fixing others to simply sitting with them in the storm.

3. **THE BLAMELESS POST-MORTEM.** "Every Friday, at this time, we are going to have a 30-minute meeting. And we are going to ask one question: 'What almost went wrong this week?' We are going to hunt for the small mistakes, the near-misses, and we are going to talk about why they happened. We will celebrate the person who finds the broken wrench, not punish them."

He capped the marker and turned to the stunned, silent team.

A senior manager, a cynic named Peters, raised his hand. "Ben, that's... admirable. But how are we supposed to maintain our billables? The clients won't care about our 'covenant' when they have a 5 PM deadline."

"They won't," Ben said. "Which is why we will be a team that is anchored, rested, and clear. We will be a team that doesn't make stupid, catastrophic, million-pound mistakes. Our new value to the client is not our burnout. It's our integrity. It's our resilience."

Tom, who had been standing at the back, spoke up. His voice was quiet, but it had a new weight. "I was the one who made the mistake. I was burned out, and I missed a date. I cost this team. I'm the reason for this. And I'm telling you... the 'buddy system' would have caught it. The 'dark' hours would have meant I wasn't too tired to see straight. This isn't soft. This is a fortress. This is how we win."

The team looked at Tom. He was not a failure. He was a survivor.

Ben looked at the group. "This isn't a suggestion. It's our new operating system. I am no longer measuring you on your hours. I'm measuring you on our integrity. Now, go home. It's 4:30. I'll see you on Monday."

They shuffled out, not in a rush, but in a daze. Confused, hopeful, skeptical.

Ben and Tom were the last ones left.

"That," Tom said, "was harder than calling Kael."

"Yeah," Ben said, erasing the whiteboard. "Because this is the real battle. Now get out of here."

Ben walked home. He didn't take a cab. He needed to feel the pavement, the solid anchor of the city. He walked for forty minutes, the noise of the traffic a strange, distant music.

He let himself into his apartment. It was quiet.

Hannah was in the living room, in the armchair, a book on her lap. She looked up when he walked in. He saw it. The familiar guard. The bracing for the storm, or the cloud, or the ghost.

He didn't give a speech. He didn't have a new, brilliant insight to present. He just... stopped.

He put his briefcase by the door.

He took off his suit jacket, folded it, and put it on the back of a chair.

He unclipped his watch and set it on the table, the metallic sound loud in the quiet room.

He walked over to the sofa and sat. He didn't crowd her. He just... sat.

He was in the room. He was just a man, home from a long week.

"Hi," he said.

"Hi," she replied. Her voice was tentative. "A... a rough couple of days?"

"Yeah," Ben said. He scrubbed his hands over his face. "It was... it was the mud. All of it."

He let out a long breath, a breath he felt like he'd been holding for three days. He was so tired. He wasn't a hero. He wasn't a guru. He was just... Ben.

He looked at her. Really looked at her.

"What are you reading?"

The question was so simple. So normal. It wasn't a diagnostic ("What are you feeling?"). It wasn't an apology ("I know I've been..."). It was just... a question.

Hannah was startled. She looked down at the book in her lap as if she'd forgotten it was there.

"Oh. It's... just a novel. About a gardener."

"Is it good?" he asked.

A small, tentative smile touched her lips. "Yeah. It's... it's quiet."

"Good," Ben said. He leaned his head back on the sofa and closed his eyes, just for a second.

He was not in the past. He was not in the future. He was on his sofa, next to his wife, and the room was quiet. He was anchored.

He opened his eyes. She was just looking at him. And the guard was gone. The shield was down. She wasn't seeing a ghost, or a cloud, or a jerk. She was just seeing... him.

"Welcome home, Ben," she whispered.

Chapter - 17
The Echo

A month passed. The adrenaline faded, as it always does, and was replaced by the simple, unglamorous rhythm of the work. The Kael deal was a legend, a story whispered by new associates, but for the 41st floor, it was just the beginning of a new, awkward, and often frustrating reality.

The "New Covenant" was not a celebration. It was friction.

"Ben, you've got a minute?"

It was Peters, the senior manager, the cynic. He was standing in Ben's doorway, his arms crossed, holding a document.

"Of course, Peters. Come in."

Peters didn't sit. He walked to the desk and dropped the proposal. "This," he said, tapping it, "is the quarterly projection for the retail group. It's a day late. Not because the work was hard. But because Tom—who's now our 'integrity buddy'—was in a 'dark hours' mandated meeting, so he couldn't sign off."

Ben felt the old, familiar clench. The "roommate" cleared his throat, enjoying the new material. *See? I told you. This 'covenant' is a joke. You're slow. You're soft. You're losing.*

Ben felt his feet on the floor. He didn't react. He just listened.

"It's not efficient, Ben," Peters continued, his voice tight with a lifetime of 90-hour weeks. "We're building a fortress, sure. But we're also building a bureaucracy. We're losing our edge. The clients want sharks, not... whatever this is."

The old Ben would have seen this as a challenge. A debate to be won. He would have argued, pulling rank.

The new Ben saw Peters. He saw a man who had built his entire identity, his entire sense of self-worth, on being a shark. He saw a man who was, in his own way, just as terrified as Tom had been.

"You're right," Ben said.

Peters stopped, mid-rant. "What?"

"You're right. It is slow. And it is inefficient. Right now."

Ben stood up, but not to loom. He came around the desk and leaned against it, putting himself on the same level.

"This," he said, picking up the proposal, "is the cost of re-tooling the factory. We were building cars with faulty bolts. We're now stopping the assembly line to fix the machines. It's a nightmare. And it's the only way."

"But Ben, the clients..."

"Peters," Ben said, "I have a new rule. I'm not running a team of sharks. Sharks get eaten. They get exhausted.

They get sloppy. I'm running a team of... engineers. We're building a system that doesn't fail. And that takes time. The friction you're feeling? It's the sign that it's working. It's the feeling of old, bad habits grinding against a new, better process."

"But I..."

"I've got a question for you," Ben said, and his voice was genuinely curious. "You're the best shark I've got. You see angles no one else does. What if you used that brain, not to tell me *why* this is slow, but to tell me how to make it *faster*... without breaking it?"

Peters was silent. He had come in for a fight, and Ben had just offered him a job. A better one.

"You're asking me to... what? Help you with this... 'covenant'?"

"I'm asking you to be the lead engineer on it," Ben said. "You're the one feeling the friction. Show me where to put the oil. We'll talk about it at the post-mortem."

Peters, disarmed and confused, just nodded. "Okay. I'll... I'll think about it." He walked out, his entire worldview subtly, violently, knocked off its axis.

Ben sat down. His "roommate" was quiet. The old Ben would have felt a surge of adrenaline from "winning" the argument. The new Ben just felt... a quiet sense of clarity. The work was done.

That night, he was on the floor of the playroom, building a lopsided tower of blocks with Leo. His son was having a full, red-faced, three-year-old tantrum because the blue block wouldn't fit.

"NO! NO! IT GOES HERE!" Leo shrieked, his whole body stiff with pure, irrational rage.

Ben felt the "Cloud" rising in him. The urge to float above it. He is just telling a story of frustration...

He felt Hannah's presence in the doorway. She was just watching them, a small, tentative smile on her face.

Ben looked at his furious, screaming son. He let the "Cloud" go. He let the "Guru" go.

He just got in the mud.

"It's SO frustrating!" Ben said, his voice full of the same energy as Leo's. "This blue block is a JERK! I hate it!"

Leo's shriek stopped, cut off by a gasp of pure shock. His father... his father understood.

"It's a JERK!" Leo agreed, his face still red, but his eyes now clear.

"What if," Ben said, "we tell the blue block he can't be in the tower? What if he's in... time out?"

Leo giggled. A real, full-belly giggle. "Blue block in time out!"

"Okay," Ben said, "let's build the tower without him."

He and his son built the tower. Hannah came in and sat on the floor with them. The "roommate" wasn't there. The "client" wasn't there. The "firm" wasn't there.

Ben Harris was just a man on a floor, building a lopsided tower with his family, in the quiet, wonderful, ordinary mud of his own life.

Chapter - 18
The Savior's Trap

The "New Covenant" became the 41st floor's new religion, and Ben was its unwilling, or perhaps all-too-willing, high priest.

The Friday "Blameless Post-Mortem" was a standing-room-only event. Ben would stand at the whiteboard, a marker in hand, and his team would, one by one, offer up their "near-misses."

"I almost sent the wrong draft to the printers for the AGM," Peters, the former cynic, confessed in front of the group.

The Old Ben would have fired him. The Cloud Ben would have observed him. The new, Engineer Ben just nodded, his face a mask of calm, constructive curiosity.

"Okay," Ben said, turning to the board. "Let's run the diagnostic. This isn't a Peters problem. This is a system problem."

He was brilliant. He was in the mud, but with a blueprint. He involved the team, asking questions that were so perfectly Socratic, so devoid of ego, that they always led to the right answer.

"So, the file-naming convention is the real villain here," he concluded, twenty minutes later. "And the 'buddy' wasn't assigned early enough in the workflow."

He looked at the team. "Great catch, Peters. You just saved us a six-figure re-print. You're a hero. Next?"

The team was in awe. They were *safe*. They were *learning*. Morale had never been higher. Productivity, after the initial dip, was climbing past its old benchmarks because the *quality* of the work was perfect. There were no more fires. Ben had become the ultimate fire marshal, the perfect systems engineer.

And his "roommate" was no longer a roommate. He was a fawning biographer.

...Look at them, Ben. They're hanging on your every word...

...Peters, that old shark, he respects you now. He'd follow you anywhere...

...You're not just a boss. You're a savior. You've built this. You are the anchor for all of them...

Ben found himself addicted to this new feeling. It was quieter than the adrenaline of the Kael deal, but deeper. It was the drug of being *needed*. Of being *wise*.

He brought this new identity home.

Hannah was in the kitchen, on the phone. Her shoulders were tense.

"No, Mom, I... I know you think that. I'm just saying... no, that's not what I mean. I just mean... she's my sister, I can't just..."

She hung up the phone with a sharp, frustrated sigh.

"Sister trouble?" Ben asked, leaning against the counter.

Hannah looked up, surprised. "Oh, hi. Yeah. Just... the same old. My mom's convinced my sister is 'taking advantage' of me over the summer vacation plans. I'm... I'm in the middle."

The Old Ben would have grunted and checked his phone.

The Cloud Ben would have said, "I'm observing you're in her story."

The new, Engineer Ben smiled. This was a system with a flaw. He could fix this.

"Okay," he said, pulling up a stool. "Let's run the diagnostic."

Hannah blinked. "Run the... what?"

"Your mom. Your sister. You're the fulcrum. What's the real 'why' here? What's your mom's actual fear?"

"What? Ben, it's just... a family thing."

"But it's a system," Ben said, warming to the topic, his voice full of the same calm, constructive energy he used in the post-mortems. "Your mom's fear of 'being taken advantage of' is the bug in the code. Your sister's defensiveness is the reaction. You're the processor, trying to run two conflicting programs at once. You're not in the mud, Han. You just need a better operating system."

He was brilliant. He was empathetic. He was *present*. He gave her a three-point plan for how to have two separate, clear conversations with her mom and her sister, setting new "protocols" for their communication.

Hannah listened. She was quiet, her head tilted. When he was done, she didn't look relieved. She looked... impressed. And a little sad.

"Wow," she said, her voice small. "That's... that's really smart, Ben. It's like... you've engineered the whole thing. A 'New Covenant' for the family."

She kissed him, but it was a quick, distant peck on the cheek. "Thank you. I... I'll think about that."

She picked up her phone and walked into the living room.

Ben stood in the kitchen. He was alone.

He had "won." He had "solved" her. And she had walked away.

The "roommate" had no words for this. The praise died in his throat.

Ben was the savior of the 41st floor. He was the wise engineer of his own home. He had achieved perfect, calm, systematic mastery.

And for the first time, he felt the old, familiar, hollow ache return. The unmistakable chill of the glass office. He had traded one performance—the Anxious Partner—for another, more sophisticated one: the Wise, Calm Engineer.

He had become the perfect guru. The perfect coach. The perfect partner.

And it was the most subtle, most complete, and most lonely performance of his life. He wasn't a jerk in the mud. He was a hero on a pedestal. And a pedestal is just a taller, smaller prison cell.

He sat down at the kitchen table. He looked at his hands. He was still, after all of it, just... Ben. A man. A man who was tired of performing.

He picked up his phone. He had one last question for Maya.

How do you stop performing? How do you just... be?

Chapter - 19
The Man on the Floor

The green door was just a door. When Maya opened it, Ben didn't bring in a storm or a cloud. He just brought Ben.

"No tea," he said, walking in. "And no coffee. I'm just... here."

"I can see that," Maya said, her eyes crinkling in a small smile. She sat in her armchair. "You've been busy."

"I fixed it," Ben said. He didn't sit. He paced. He told her everything. The Kael deal. The "New Covenant." The blameless post-mortems. The way he had converted Peters, the cynic, into an engineer of the new system. He was proud. He laid out his achievements like a general laying out battle maps.

"And Tom?" she asked.

"Tom is... great," Ben said, a flash of genuine pride. "He's a new man. He's a leader. The system works, Maya. It's strong. It's resilient. I... I fixed the machine."

"That's wonderful," Maya said. Her voice was perfectly even. "And yet, you're here. You're pacing. The war is over, Ben. Why is the soldier still in his armor?"

Ben stopped pacing. He looked at the wall of books, his back to her.

"I went home," he said, his voice dropping. "And I... I tried to fix that, too."

He explained the scene with Hannah. The fight with her sister. His "diagnosis." His "system-fix." His perfect, empathetic, brilliant engineering of her family problems.

And then he told her the result. The sad, impressed look in her eyes. The distant peck on the cheek. The hollow, quiet loneliness of his victory.

"She walked away," he said. "She was... sad. I gave her the perfect answer, and it just... pushed her away. I've become the best leader, the best coach, the best engineer... and I've never been more alone."

He turned to face her. The last performance had crumbled. He was just a man.

"I'm exhausted," he said, his voice raw. "I'm exhausted from performing. First, I was the Anxious Partner. Then I was the Detached Guru. Now I'm the Wise, Calm Savior. And it's all just... a costume. It's the best one I've ever had, Maya. It's the one my ego loves the most. And it's just... another glass office."

He finally sank into the armchair. The fight was gone.

"How do I stop?" he whispered. "How do I stop... performing? How do I just... be?"

Maya was quiet for a long, long time. She just looked at him, with a gaze that was not a diagnosis, not an observation, but just... a human seeing another human.

"You can't," she said.

"What?"

"You can't try to stop performing. 'Not performing' just becomes your new performance. The 'authentic guy' becomes your new costume. The ego is a brilliant costume designer, Ben. It will always find a new outfit."

"So I'm trapped?" he said, feeling a chill. "This is it? I'm just a series of performances until I die?"

"No," she said, a small smile playing on her lips. "You're just looking for the 'fix' in the wrong place. You're still trying to *engineer* your way out. You're trying to find a system for authenticity."

"Then what's the answer?"

"You're asking the wrong question," she said. "You're asking 'How do *I* do this?' That's the trap. The 'I' is the performance. You've been so focused on being the anchor for everyone else. The strong one. The calm one. The engineer with the plan."

She leaned in. "What would happen... if you just... fell apart?"

"What?"

"What would happen if, when Hannah was in her storm, you didn't have a plan? What if you didn't have an answer? What if you just said, 'God, that sounds... awful. I don't know what to do, but I'm here'?"

Ben was silent. The thought was terrifying.

"That's... not leading," he said. "That's... weakness."

"Is it?" Maya asked. "Or is it just... true? You're the engineer who fixed the firm. But you're also the man who is terrified of not having the answer. You're the man who is lonely in his own kitchen. You're not a savior, Ben. You're just a man."

She stood up. "Your 'roommate'... your 'anchor'... your 'umbrella'... these were all just tools, Ben. Tools to get you back to the present moment. Tools to get you out of the storm in your own head."

"But what do I do in the present moment?" he pleaded.

"You stop asking that question!" she said, and for the first time, there was a sharp, bright fire in her voice. "You stop trying to 'do' the present moment! You just... *live* it."

"When you're with Tom, be the engineer. When you're with Leo, be the monster. And when you're with Hannah, and she's in pain... don't be her guru. Be her partner. Be as confused and messy and human as she is. Stop bringing your armor home from the office."

She walked to the door.

"This is our last session, Ben."

"What? No. I... I'm not fixed."

"You are not a machine, Ben. You don't get fixed. You're just... Ben. You have all the tools. You know what the roommate is. You know where the anchor is. You know how to bring an umbrella."

She smiled, a real, warm, goodbye smile.

"Your problem isn't that you don't know what to do. Your problem is that you think there's a 'right' way to do it. There isn't. There's just... being. Go be a man on the floor, building a lopsided tower. Go be a husband who just... listens. Go be a boss who is, sometimes, just as confused as everyone else. Stop trying to be the anchor for the whole world. Just be the anchor for your own two feet. The rest... it's just a dance."

Ben stood up. He felt... light. He felt... terrified. He felt... just... Ben.

He walked to the door.

"Thank you, Maya."

"Go get in the mud, Ben," she said.

He walked out of the green door for the last time. He didn't have a plan. He didn't have a new performance.

He was just a man, walking in the afternoon sun, his hands in his pockets, finally, wonderfully, just... home.

Chapter - 20
The Man in the Kitchen

He walked through his front door. It was 6:00 PM. The time of domestic chaos.

He could hear it from the hallway. Leo was in full-blown tantrum mode, not a "frustrated-by-a-block" tantrum, but the high-pitched, world-ending shriek of a small human who is overtired and over-sugared. And in the kitchen, there was the sound of a pot lid clattering to the floor.

The "roommate" surfaced, an old, familiar reflex. *God, I'm exhausted. I just want quiet. This is her job, why is it always so...*

The "Engineer" surfaced, right behind him. *Okay. System failure. Triage: first, calm the child. Second, assist the partner. Third, assess the meal...*

The "Cloud" just wanted to float away to a quiet room and *observe* the noise.

Ben stood in his hallway, his hand still on the doorknob. He was a crowded, messy, walking contradiction. He was all of these things. He was not a guru. He was not a failure. He was just a tired man, home from a long day.

He took a breath. He felt his feet on the floor. Not to anchor himself *away* from the chaos, but to anchor himself *in* it. He dropped his briefcase. He rolled up his sleeves. He was home.

He walked into the kitchen.

It was a beautiful disaster. Hannah was at the stove, her back to him, one hand stirring a pot while the other was wiping spilled pasta sauce off the counter. Leo was on the floor, a small, red-faced god of thunder, hammering a wooden spoon against a cabinet.

"I DON'T WANT IT!" Leo screamed, a tear-streaked face turned up to the heavens.

"You don't even know what 'it' is!" Hannah snapped, her voice frayed to a single, thin wire. She slammed the spoon down, splattering more sauce. "I don't... I just... I cannot do this right now!"

She saw Ben.

Her face, which was angry and frustrated, instantly froze. The shield went up. She was bracing for his performance. For the irritable partner. For the cold, diagnosing guru.

"I'm sorry," she said, her voice instantly flat and formal. "It's been a day. Leo missed his nap. I'll get him quiet."

Ben looked at the chaos. He looked at his son, who was a tiny ball of pure, unfiltered rage. He looked at his wife, who was a tight, wound-up coil of exhaustion and loneliness.

He didn't have a plan. He didn't have a system. He was just as tired as she was.

So he just got in the mud.

He walked past Hannah, went to the cabinet, and grabbed a wooden spoon.

He walked over to Leo. He didn't try to calm him. He didn't observe him.

He sat down on the floor, cross-legged, in his expensive suit trousers.

He looked his son in the eye.

"YOU'RE RIGHT!" Ben shouted, his voice a low, theatrical roar.

Leo's scream hitched in his throat. He stopped, his spoon in mid-air, utterly baffled.

"THIS IS AWFUL!" Ben yelled, and he banged his own spoon on the floor, right next to Leo's. BANG! "THIS SAUCE IS... TOO... RED! THIS FLOOR IS... TOO... HARD!"

BANG! BANG!

A tiny, confused smile flickered on Leo's face. He looked at his dad. He looked at his spoon.

He raised it.

BANG! went Leo.

BANG! went Ben.

BANG! BANG! BANG!

They sat on the floor, a partner at one of London's top firms and a three-year-old, having a full-blown, orchestral tantrum together, pounding out a furious, ridiculous, joyful rhythm of protest against... nothing.

After a minute, they were both laughing. A gasping, breathless, silly laugh. Ben was covered in sauce. Leo had a noodle in his hair.

Ben looked up at Hannah.

She was leaning against the counter, her hands over her mouth. Her shoulders were shaking. She was crying. But this time, she was smiling. It was the first time he had seen her really, truly smile in... he couldn't remember.

He stood up, his knees cracking. He was just a man, on the floor, covered in pasta.

He walked over to his wife.

She didn't brace. She didn't put up a shield.

He just... put his arms around her. He didn't say, "You should be calm." He didn't say, "Let's fix this." He just... held her. He held her, and the smell of jasmine tea and old books, of rage and pasta sauce, all of it, was just... real.

She buried her face in his shirt.

"God, Ben," she whispered into his chest. "You're a mess."

"Yeah," he said, his own voice thick, as he held her. "I know. I'm... I'm finally, really in the mud."

He felt her smile against his shirt.

"Welcome home," she said.

He closed his eyes. The "roommate" was silent. The "engineer" was off duty. The "guru" had left the building.

There was no glass office. There was no performance.

There was just the anchor. And this time, it was a shared one. It was just a man in a kitchen, holding his wife, a small boy tugging at his trousers.

He was home.

Chapter - 21
The Man in the Armor

The new system, the Covenant, was humming. The floor was no longer a high-pressure burn unit; it was a focused, resilient, and strangely calm engineering lab. The "Blameless Post-Mortems" had become the most valuable meeting of the week, a session of collective, ego-free problem-solving.

Ben was at his desk. It was a normal Tuesday. He was... working. Just working. His "roommate" was now just a normal thought process, not a tyrant. His anchor was just... his feet. It had all become, thankfully, wonderfully, *normal.*

His door was open. It was always open now.

"Ben?"

Peters was standing in the doorway.

"Hey, Peters," Ben said, looking up from his screen. "What's the fire?"

But there was no fire. Peters, the sharp, cynical, newly-converted engineer of the new system... he was ashen. He looked old. His armor, the sharp suit and the sharper sarcasm, was gone. He looked like a man who hadn't slept in a week.

"Peters? What is it? Come in."

Peters walked in and sat in the chair opposite Ben's desk. He just... sat. He stared at the floor.

Ben felt the familiar, old-world "Boss" instinct. Okay, what's the problem, let's solve it, I've got a 2PM call.

He felt the "Engineer" instinct. Okay, what's the system failure? Workload? Team friction?

He pushed them both aside. He just... waited. He brought an umbrella, and he waited for the rain.

"I..." Peters began, and his voice was a dry rasp. "I don't know why I'm here."

"Okay," Ben said. He just sat, hands open on his desk. He was not a guru. He was just a man in a room.

"The... the Covenant," Peters said, a bitter, hollow laugh. "It's... it's a hell of a thing, Ben."

"It's working, isn't it?"

"Oh, yeah. It's working. It's working perfectly. I've never... I've never been so efficient. I'm... I'm home by 6:30 every night. Every single night."

"That's... good, right?"

Peters finally looked up. His eyes were red-rimmed and hollow.

"She's leaving me, Ben."

The words hung in the air, a different kind of bomb.

"What?"

"My wife," Peters said, his voice breaking, the shark finally, utterly, gone. "She's... she told me last night. She wants a divorce. She said... she said 'Congratulations on your new, efficient life. It's a little late.' She said... for twenty years, I've been a... a 'ghost who pays the bills.' And now that I'm finally home... there's no one there. She's... she's just done. She's been done for years. I was just too busy to notice."

Ben's "roommate" screamed. DANGER! HR VIOLATION! NOT YOUR PROBLEM! ABORT!

The "Engineer" raced for a fix. Okay, marriage counseling. EAP. We have systems for this!

Ben did nothing. He just sat. He just... heard it. He was in the mud. And it was deep.

"God, Peters," Ben said. His voice was just his voice. "That's... awful. I... I'm so sorry."

There was no wisdom. There was no cloud. There was just a man in a room, with another man who was falling apart.

Peters was crying now. Silent, awful, shoulder-shaking tears. The shark, the cynic, the man who lived in armor, was just... gone.

"I don't know what to do," Peters whispered, his face in his hands. "I fixed everything. I'm... I'm the lead engineer, right? I'm... I'm following the system. I'm doing it all right. And my life... my life... is over. I'm a... I'm an efficient, empty... suit."

He looked at Ben, his eyes desperate. "You're the guy, Ben. You're the one who... you fixed this whole floor. You saved Tom. You saved Kael. You've got the answers. Fix *me*. What's the system? What's the... what's the Covenant for *this*?"

He was offering Ben the crown. He was offering him the "Savior" costume. The most powerful, most seductive costume of all. *Fix me. Be my guru.*

Ben looked at this broken, powerful, brilliant man. He looked at his own hands. He felt his feet on the floor. He remembered Maya's last, greatest lesson. *You're not a machine. You don't get fixed.*

Ben let out a long, slow breath.

"I can't, Peters."

Peters's face fell.

"I don't have an answer," Ben said. He leaned forward on his desk, his hands open. "I don't have a fix. I don't have a... a Covenant for this. It's... it's just... the real, terrible mud. I... I don't know what to do."

Peters stared, his tears slowing. He was confused.

"But... you're..."

"I'm just a guy, Peters," Ben said, a small, sad smile. "I'm just a guy in a suit, just like you, trying to figure it out. I'm not a guru. I'm just... the guy in the next office."

Ben stood up. He walked to the small fridge in his office, took out two bottles of water, and sat down, not behind his desk, but in the guest chair, right next to Peters. He handed him one.

"I can't fix it," Ben said, his voice a low rumble, sitting shoulder-to-shoulder with him. "I don't have a plan. But... I can sit here. This... this is a mess. And you're not in it alone."

Peters just held the cold bottle of water. He was still crying, but the panic was gone. He was just... a man, in a room, with another man.

"That's it?" Peters whispered.

"That's it," Ben said. "That's all I've got."

Ben looked at his watch. "Here's the new plan. You're taking the rest of the week off. Effective now."

"Ben, I can't, the projections..."

"I'm not asking. I'm telling. The system," Ben said, with a small, knowing look, "will cover you. Tom and I will cover you. That's why we built the damn thing. Not to be more efficient. But to be more human. To give us the space to... to break, and to know that the machine will keep running. Go. Go home. Don't... don't try to fix anything. Just... go be in your house. Be a... a man in a room. I'll call you Friday."

Peters stood up. He looked at his boss. His... friend.

"Okay, Ben."

"Okay, Peters."

Peters walked out, for the first time, without his armor.

Ben stayed in the chair. He looked at the empty seat next to him.

The "roommate" was silent. The "engineer" was quiet.

He was just Ben. And that, he was finally learning, was more than enough.

Chapter - 22
The Man Who Said No

Three months later. The Covenant was no longer new. It was just... the way things were. The 41st floor was, by a strange and quiet metric, the most stable and high-performing division in the London office. The error rate was zero. Attrition was zero.

A calendar invite appeared on Ben's screen.

"Annual Performance Review: Ben Harris."

The sender: Sarah.

The old Ben would have spent three days preparing a deck, practicing his "wins," and spiraling in anxiety.

The "roommate" did, in fact, show up for a brief, nostalgic performance.

...This is it! The Kael bonus! They're probably going to promote you! Remember to mention the new efficiency stats...

Ben heard the voice. He smiled, a small, private smile.

"Thinking," he labeled it, and went back to his email.

He walked into her office at 3:00 PM. No deck. No notes. Just... Ben.

Sarah was at her desk, the first time he'd seen her not in a conference room. Her office was, predictably, a masterpiece of minimalist power.

"Ben," she said, motioning to the chair. "Close the door."

That was never good. He sat.

"The Kael deal," she said, no preamble. "Was a legend. The bonus reflect-a-that."

"Thank you, Sarah."

"But that's not what we're here to talk about," she said, steepling her fingers. "We're here to talk about your numbers."

"Okay."

"Your team's billable hours are down, year-over-year, by eight percent. Your team's revenue, however, is up by four percent. And your error and attrition rate is at zero."

She paused, letting the numbers hang in the air.

"It's a... confusing dashboard, Ben. The other partners, they see the 8% drop in billables, and they get nervous. They see 'dark hours' and 'buddy systems' as... soft. As inefficient."

"They're not," Ben said simply.

"I know," Sarah said, a sharp look in her eye. "I'm the one who's been defending it. I'm the one who showed the board that your 'soft' system saved us from a 500-million-pound lawsuit and netted us a new contract with Kael. What I want to know is... what is this? What did Maya do to you?"

Ben felt his feet on the floor. He didn't have a performance. He didn't have a spin. He just had the truth.

"She... she just helped me get out of my own way, Sarah. She helped me see that I was at war with my own mind, and I was making the team a casualty of that war. The Covenant... it's not a 'system,' not really. It's just... it's just a set of rules to make it safe for people to be human."

Sarah looked at him for a long, long time. She was seeing the man she'd sent to a coach, a man who had been a hollow, vibrating mess of anxiety. And she was seeing the man in front of her. Calm. Anchored. Solid.

"Well," she said, leaning back. "The board is impressed. Kael is... Kael is now your biggest advocate, which is terrifying. And they see an opportunity."

She slid a single, thick document across the desk.

"They're opening a new global division. Head of Global Risk and Resilience. It's not a legal job. It's a... a systems job. A human systems job. They want someone to take the 'New Covenant' and apply it. Firm-wide."

She looked at him. "This... this is a Managing Director role, Ben. It's the big chair. It's yours. If you want it."

This was it. The ultimate crown. The biggest, most glorious glass office of all.

The "roommate" was apoplectic, screaming with joy. THIS IS IT! WE'VE WON! MD! GLOBAL!

The "Engineer" was already designing the new, global post-mortem protocols.

The "Savior" was ready to fix the entire, broken world.

Ben looked at the document. He saw the title. He saw the corner office on the 60th floor. He saw the flights to Singapore. He saw the 80-hour weeks, the performance reviews, the pressure, the... *performance*.

And then he looked out the window. He thought of the 41st floor. He thought of Tom, who was now mentoring a new associate. He thought of Peters, who was back from his leave and was, awkwardly, clumsily, trying to reconnect with his wife, and who, for the first time, had been honest about it at work.

He thought of Hannah's smile. He thought of the weight of Leo, asleep on his chest. He thought of the mud.

He slid the document back across the desk.

"No, thank you, Sarah."

Sarah's jaw, for the first time Ben had ever seen, dropped.

"...I'm sorry, I... did you say no?"

"It's an incredible honor," Ben said, and he meant it. "And a year ago, I would have killed for it. But... I don't want it."

"You don't want... Ben, this is a career-defining promotion."

"I know," Ben said, and a real, warm, genuine smile touched his lips. "But I... I'm not an engineer for the whole firm. I'm just a partner on the 41st floor. I'm... I'm finally learning how to do that job. How to be a partner. How to be a... a husband. A father."

He stood up. He felt light. He felt free.

"I'm not a savior, Sarah. I'm not a guru. I'm just... Ben. I've got a blameless post-mortem at 4, and I promised my wife I'd be home for dinner. And I... I really, really don't want to be late."

He stood in front of his boss. He was not a subordinate. He was not an achiever. He was just... a man, anchored.

Sarah stared at him. The shark, the cynic, the high-stakes corporate warrior.

And she smiled. A real, brilliant, surprised smile. The man in front of her had just been offered the kingdom, and he had turned it down for... his own life. He was the only sane man in the building.

"Go," she said, a new, deep respect in her voice. "Get out of here. And Ben?"

"Yeah?"

"Good work."

"You too, Sarah."

Ben walked out of her office. He walked past the 60th-floor elevators. He got in the lift, went down to the 41st, and stepped out into the familiar, quiet hum of his own team.

He was just a man in an office.

He was just Ben.

Chapter - 23
The Man with the Umbrella

Life settled into a new, sustainable rhythm. The "New Covenant" was no longer a revolution; it was just the way they worked. Ben's days were still long, still full of pressure, but the quality of the pressure had changed. It was the focused, creative tension of solving a problem, not the frantic, corrosive anxiety of managing a performance.

He was home for dinner. He was present for his wife. He was on the floor with his son. He was, for the most part, just Ben.

One Tuesday, his phone buzzed. It was an unknown number.

"Ben Harris."

"Mr. Harris?" The voice was professional, but hesitant. "My name is Alice. I... I'm Dr. Aris's assistant."

Ben's anchor dropped. He stood up from his desk and walked to the glass wall. "Maya? Is she alright?"

"I'm... I'm not sure," Alice's voice was strained. "She... she was supposed to be in sessions all day. She didn't show up. She's not answering her phone. I used the spare key to check on her apartment, and she... she's there.

She's fine. Physically. But she... she won't come to the door. She just told me to go away."

"What happened?" Ben asked, a cold knot forming in his stomach.

"Her... her ex-husband. He passed away. Two days ago. A sudden heart attack. They've been divorced for twenty years, but... I don't know. She just... she's not herself. I don't know who else to call. She spoke about you once. She said you were 'an engineer who learned to get in the mud.' I... I think she's in the mud, Mr. Harris. I'm worried."

Ben was out of the office in five minutes.

He stood in front of the familiar green door in the Marylebone alley. It felt different. It was no longer a door to a sanctuary. It was just a door. He knocked.

"Go away, Alice! I'm fine!" Her voice was thick, muffled, and anything but fine.

"It's not Alice," Ben said, his voice steady. "It's Ben. Ben Harris. I'm... I'm here."

There was a long, deep silence. He could hear a faint shuffling.

The door opened, just a crack.

The woman who looked through the gap was not Maya, the guru. She was not the calm, centered anchor.

She was a small, pale woman in a rumpled bathrobe, her hair uncombed, her eyes red and swollen. She was... just a woman. A woman who was grieving.

"Ben?" she said, her voice a small, cracked thing.

"Hi, Maya."

She just stared at him, as if she couldn't quite place him in this new context.

"You... you shouldn't be here," she whispered. "I'm... I'm not... I'm a mess."

The "Engineer" in Ben's head raced to find a fix. Okay, grief protocol. Step 1: Acknowledge loss. Step 2: Offer support. Step 3: Assess needs...

The "Savior" wanted to give her a lecture. Maya, you are just experiencing a story of loss. You are the sky, this is just a cloud...

He felt his feet on the floor. He saw the woman in front of him. His teacher. His mentor. His friend. And she was in pain.

He didn't have a plan. He didn't have a system. He just... got in the mud.

"You are a mess," he said, his voice full of a gentle, simple warmth. "It's... it's awful. I'm... I'm so sorry."

He didn't wait for an invitation. He just gently pushed the door open, stepped inside, and closed it behind him, shutting out the rest of the world.

The quiet, perfect office was a disaster. Teacups were everywhere. Tissues were on the floor. The books were in disarray.

"I... I don't understand," Maya said, her voice trembling as she shuffled back to the armchair. "We... we haven't spoken in ten years. Not really. Why... why does this hurt so much? I'm... I'm supposed to be... I'm supposed to know better."

She looked at him, her eyes desperate, the student's eyes. "I'm... I'm lost in the storm, Ben. I can't find my anchor. I can't... I can't find the sky. It's just... all storm."

She was offering him the crown. Save me. Be my guru.

Ben looked at this brilliant, broken woman. He thought of Hannah in the kitchen. He thought of Peters in his office.

He did not sit in the other chair.

He walked into her small kitchenette. He found the kettle. He found the jasmine tea. His hands moved with a simple, quiet purpose.

He made two cups of tea, just as she had done for him all those months ago.

He came back. He handed her one. He sat, not in the other armchair, but on the floor, leaning his back against the bookshelf, just as he had done in his living room with Hannah.

He was not her equal. He was not her student. He was not her savior.

He was just... a man in the room.

"It hurts," he said, his voice a low rumble. "Because it was real. Because you're human."

He sipped his tea. "You don't have to 'know better' today, Maya. You just... you just have to hurt. It's... it's just the mud."

She looked at him over the rim of her teacup. Her hands were shaking.

"But I'm... I'm the one... I'm the lighthouse," she whispered.

"I know," Ben said. "But even lighthouses get hit by waves. You're just... you're in the wave. It's okay."

He didn't offer a protocol. He didn't offer a fix. He didn't offer her own wisdom back to her.

He just... sat.

He sat with her, on the floor, in the messy, human, heartbreaking mud of her grief.

He brought his umbrella.

And he sat with her, in the storm, until it passed.

He was just... Ben. And he was, finally, completely, home.

Chapter - 24
The Man in the Room

The alarm on Ben's phone went off at 6:00 AM.

He didn't hit snooze. He just reached over, turned it off, and didn't pick up the phone.

He just lay there, in the pre-dawn dark.

He felt the sheets on his skin. He heard the faint, distant hum of the city beginning to wake. He heard the soft, deep breathing of Hannah beside him.

He wasn't labeling. He wasn't observing. He wasn't anchoring.

He was just... awake.

He was just... here.

He slipped out of bed, walked into the kitchen, and started the coffee. He sat at the kitchen table for ten minutes. He didn't meditate. He didn't check his email. He just sat, in the dark, and drank a cup of coffee. He watched the light in the sky change from gray to a pale, hopeful blue.

He was just a man, in a kitchen, watching the sun rise.

At 7:00 AM, the house was a storm. A beautiful, glorious storm. Leo was shouting about his socks.

Hannah was trying to find a permission slip. The "roommate" in Ben's head was muttering about the 9 AM projection meeting.

"Dad! Dad! The red sock is BAD! I need the BLUE!" Leo shrieked, a small, perfect storm of three-year-old rage.

Ben, who was trying to butter toast with one hand and sign the permission slip with the other, just laughed. He looked at Hannah, who was also laughing. Their eyes met over the top of their son's furious head. It was the look of two partners, in the same boat, in the same mud.

"You're right, Leo," Ben said, kneeling. "The red sock is a JERK. Let's go find the blue one."

He slung Leo over his shoulder and carried him, still shrieking, out of the kitchen.

He walked into the 41st floor at 8:50 AM. It was... calm. People were talking by the coffee machine. There was a low, productive hum.

The 4:00 PM "Blameless Post-Mortem" was no longer in Ben's office. It was in the main conference room. Ben sat at the back, not at the head of the table.

Tom was at the whiteboard. He was no longer the trembling kid. He was a calm, confident, 30-year-old leader, running the meeting.

"Okay," Tom said, "Peters found this one. It's a 'near-miss' on the new client intake. Peters?"

Peters stood up. His armor was gone. He was just... Peters. He was still a shark, but he was a shark that was now protecting the team, not just himself.

"The 'buddy system' caught it," Peters said. "The client's primary address was entered, but the secondary billing address wasn't. The old system would have let it slide. The new one flagged it. A two-second fix that saved us a two-week billing nightmare. The why... the system flaw... is that the intake form isn't clear enough. The two fields look the same."

"Great catch," Tom said. "Okay, new action item: I'll work with IT to re-design the UI on that form. What's next?"

Ben just... sat. He listened. He was, in the best possible way, redundant. He had engineered a system that no longer needed him to be the hero. He had built leaders.

At 5:30, a real fire landed on his desk. A client, a mid-level one, was pulling their account. An unexpected, no-warning, "we're leaving" email.

The old Ben would have felt a spike of hot, personal failure.

The Cloud Ben would have observed the failure.

The Engineer Ben would have called a panic meeting.

Ben Harris just read the email. He felt the familiar, cold jolt of "This is bad."

He felt his feet on the floor.

He picked up his phone. He didn't call the client. He didn't call Sarah.

He called Tom.

"Hey, you still here? Good. Grab Peters. Meet me in my office. We've got a fire."

He hung up.

The two men walked in and stood in front of his desk.

"What's up?" Tom asked.

"Meyers-Briggs just pulled their account," Ben said, forwarding the email. "It's a clean break. No warning."

He watched them. Tom, the new leader, his face set, thoughtful. Peters, the cynic-turned-engineer, his eyes already narrowing, scanning for the "why."

"Okay," Tom said. "It's a failure. Let's run the diagnostic. Why? Did we miss a deadline? Was it a pricing issue? Was it me?"

"No," Peters said, his voice sharp. "It's not us. Look at the date. Their new fiscal year. This is a budget cut, disguised as a 'strategy shift.' They're just cleaning house."

"You're right," Ben said. "So. This isn't a post-mortem. This is a new strategy. What's the play? Do we fight for them?"

The three of them stood there. Not as a boss and his subordinates. But as three engineers, looking at a broken machine.

"No," Tom said. "We don't fight. We let them go. With grace. We send them a letter thanking them for their business and telling them the door is always open. It's the 'New Covenant.' We don't cling. We don't perform."

"And," Peters added, a small, shark-like smile, "we send a note to our contact at Kael's firm, letting him know that Meyers-Briggs is now... 'in play.' Let him poach them. It's a good look for us. We're partners."

Ben looked at them. He had nothing to add. They had built the new reality.

"Good," Ben said. "That's the play. Write it up. I'm going home."

He left them in his office, already working, a team of anchors.

He packed his bag. He looked at his desk. It was just a desk.

He walked to the glass wall. He looked out at the city. It was no longer a map of his success, or a symbol of his isolation.

It was just... the view. It was beautiful.

He turned off the light. He walked out of the office. He was not a savior. He was not a hero. He was not a guru.

He was just a man, walking to the elevator, a man who had finally learned to be in the mud, to bring an umbrella, and to go home to his own life.

He was just Ben. And he was free.

(The End)

Epilogue

Two Years Later

It was a Saturday. A cool, bright morning in late September.

Ben Harris was on his knees, in the mud.

He was wearing a faded t-shirt he'd owned since university and jeans stained with grass. He and Leo were waging a serious, strategic war against a stubborn patch of weeds in their small, unruly garden. Leo, now five, was the "Captain of the Trowels," and he was taking his duty very seriously.

"This one is a BAD guy!" Leo yelled, wrestling with a deep root. "He's a very bad guy," Ben agreed, his hands deep in the cool, dark earth. "He's a... he's a pirate." "A JERK pirate!" Leo giggled.

The "roommate" in Ben's head, the one who used to run the show, offered a quiet observation. *Peters's quarterly numbers are due on Monday. You should probably check your email.*

Ben heard the thought. He didn't label it. He didn't fight it. He just... let it pass by, like a cloud in the new, clear sky. The thought had no anchor, no hook. It just drifted away, dissolved by the more immediate, more real sensation of the earth on his hands and the sound of his son's laughter.

Peters was fine. Peters was now the lead engineer of the 41st floor, a shark who had learned to build systems instead of just hunt in them. Tom was his number two. The machine they had built together ran itself.

The sliding glass door opened. Hannah walked out onto the small patio, holding two cups of coffee. She wore a thick wool sweater, her feet bare. She didn't say anything. She just sat on the steps and put one of the cups down for Ben.

He saw her, and his heart gave a small, quiet, familiar thud of... *home.* He sat back on his heels, wiping his muddy hands on his jeans. He picked up the cup.

"You missed a spot," she said, nodding at a defiant weed by his foot. "I'm leaving it," Ben said, sipping the coffee. "It's… it's got character." She laughed. A real, easy laugh. It was the sound of the house.

His phone, sitting on the patio table, buzzed. A single text message lit up the screen. It was from Tom. *Client signed. We're good. Have a great weekend.*

Ben read it. He smiled. He didn't reply. He didn't need to. He set the phone, face down, on the table.

He looked at his wife, who was smiling at him over her cup. He looked at his son, who was now explaining, in great detail, why a worm was his new best friend. The "roommate" was silent. The "engineer" was off duty. The "savior" was long gone. There was no glass office. There was no performance.

There was just a man, in his garden, covered in mud, drinking his coffee, in the middle of his own, real, and perfectly lopsided life.

He sipped his coffee. He was home.

A Note on the Practices
The Anchor and the Umbrella

Ben's journey from the glass office to the garden is a story, but the tools he learned are real. They are not philosophical ideas. They are simple, practical, and potent techniques for navigating the noise of the modern world and the chaos of our own minds.

You do not need to find a "Maya." The wisdom you need is already within you. These practices are simply ways to clear away the debris of anxiety, ego, and distraction so you can hear your own, true voice.

This is not another test to "achieve" or "perform." This is just a set of keys. Use them. Be patient. Be kind to yourself. And welcome home.

1. The Roommate & The Two-Word Label

The Concept: You have a roommate in your head. Ben had one. We all do. It is the constant, unceasing inner narrator, the voice that provides commentary on your entire life. It is the voice that is, right now, reading these words and forming an opinion on them. It lives in two places: the past (which it fills with guilt and regret) and the future (which it fills with anxiety and fear).

The Problem: The "roommate" is not your friend. It is a frantic, critical, and terrified survival mechanism. And its greatest trick is that it has convinced you that it is *you*. We are fused with this voice. We think we *are* our anxiety. We think we *are* our critical thoughts. We are at war with a voice in our head, and we don't even realize we are not the voice, but the one who is *listening* to it.

The Practice: "Thinking" The first step to freedom is not to fight the roommate, but to simply see it. This was Ben's first, and most powerful, lesson.

1. The next time you feel a surge of anxiety, anger, or self-criticism, **pause**.
2. **Listen** to the specific sentence the roommate is shouting. (e.g., "You're going to fail this presentation," or "You were so stupid to say that.")
3. Then, silently and gently, with no judgment, label the entire storm with just one word: **"Thinking."**

Why It Works: The moment you label the thought, you have performed a profound act of magic. You have separated yourself from it. You are no longer *lost* in the thought; you are the *observer* of the thought.

You cannot be both the storm and the sky at the same time. This practice moves you, for a single, liberating moment, from being the storm to being the sky, calmly watching the "thinking" (the cloud) drift by. This is the beginning of all peace.

2. The Anchor

The Concept:

Ben's first breakthrough was "labeling," which showed him he was lost in his mind. His second was discovering how to get out. He learned that while the "roommate" lives in the imaginary worlds of Yesterday and Tomorrow, your body lives in only one place: Here and Now.

The Problem:

You cannot "think" your way out of anxiety. Why? Because the "roommate" is the one doing the thinking. Trying to out-think your anxiety is like trying to put out a fire with gasoline. The harder you try, the more fuel you give the fire. You get lost in observing your thoughts, becoming a "cloud" floating above your own life, rather than a participant in it.

The Practice: "Anchoring"

The solution is not to fight the mind, but to drop out of it entirely. You do this by moving your attention from your frantic thinking to your direct, physical sensing.

1. The moment you feel yourself lost in a storm of anxiety, regret, or worry (Yesterday or Tomorrow), your task is to **physically arrive** in the present.

2. Choose a simple, physical anchor. Do not just think about it; *feel* it.

   - **Feel your feet on the floor.** Notice the pressure in your heels, the fabric of your socks against your toes. Feel the solid ground holding you up.

- **Feel your hands on the desk.** Notice the cool, smooth wood or glass. Notice the grain.
- **Feel a teacup in your hand.** Notice the warmth. Notice the smooth ceramic.

3. Bring your full, undivided attention to that simple, physical sensation for just **three seconds**.

Why It Works:

It is neurologically impossible for your brain to be 100% focused on a direct, physical sensation and 100% lost in anxious thought at the same time.

For those three seconds, you have pulled your mind out of the fantasy of the past or future and anchored it in the rock-solid reality of the **Now**. The roommate starves in the Now. You are not floating. You are not lost. You are home. This is the simple, profound, physical act of being present.

3. The Umbrella

The Concept:

Ben's first two lessons were about saving himself. He learned to be the "sky" to his own storm. But when he turned this new, powerful tool on other people, it became a weapon. He became a "cloud," floating above them, calmly observing their pain. Or he became an "engineer," diagnosing their feelings as a system to be fixed. Both were just a colder, more sophisticated way of being absent.

The Problem:

When a person is in an emotional storm—scared, angry, or grieving—they do not need a guru to tell them their feelings are an illusion. And they do not need an engineer to give them a three-point plan to "fix" their sadness.

Telling someone how to fix their feeling is not empathy. It is a subtle form of judgment. It says, "Your feeling is a problem, and I am here to solve it so I can be more comfortable." It is another performance of the ego, the "Savior," and it leaves the other person feeling diagnosed, managed, and completely alone.

The Practice: "Bringing an Umbrella"

The practice of "The Umbrella" is the shift from fixing to listening. It is the decision to get in the mud with them, but to bring your own anchor. You are not there to stop their rain; you are there to sit with them in it, so they are not alone.

1. **Resist the Urge to Fix.** The next time someone comes to you in distress, your first, most important job is to fight your own internal "engineer." Do not offer advice. Do not say, "You know what you should do..."
2. **Validate Their Feeling.** Your first words should be a simple, human acknowledgment.
    - *"That sounds... awful."*

- *"I can hear how much pain you're in."*
- *"Thank you for trusting me with this."*

3. **Get Genuinely Curious.** Ask simple, open-ended questions that are not designed to find a solution, but to understand their experience.
   - *"What is that like for you right now?"*
   - *"Tell me more about what happened."*
4. **Hold the Space.** Just be there. Be quiet. Be the anchor. Your calm, non-judgmental presence is the "umbrella." It is a powerful, silent declaration that says, "You are not alone in this. I am right here. You are safe."

Why It Works:

People do not heal or solve their problems because we give them the right advice. They heal and solve their problems because we give them a safe enough space to find their own answers. The Umbrella is not about being a savior. It is about being a partner. It is the most profound act of human connection and the true essence of leadership.

4. The Blameless Post-Mortem

The Concept:

Ben's team was trapped in a culture of fear. When a mistake happened, the first, unconscious question everyone asked was, "Whose fault is this?" This created a team of "ghosts" and "performers" who spent more energy hiding their mistakes than they did solving them.

The Problem:

In a culture of blame, you never hear about a problem when it's small. You only hear about it when it's a catastrophe. People are not incentivized to find and flag small errors; they are incentivized to bury them, hoping they go away. The "roommate" (ego) of each team member is terrified of being seen as a failure. This fear-based system doesn't prevent mistakes; it just guarantees that the mistakes you do have will be catastrophic.

The Practice: "The 'New Covenant' System"

This practice is an agreement—a "covenant"—with your team to change the rules of the game. It shifts the focus from the person to the process. It assumes that everyone is smart, capable, and trying to do their best. Therefore, when a mistake happens, it is not a human failure; it is a system failure.

1. **Schedule the Ritual:** Create a regular, mandatory meeting (like Ben's "Blameless Post-Mortem") with the sole purpose of asking one question: **"What almost went wrong this week?"**

2. **Hunt for "Near-Misses":** You must celebrate the person who brings a small error or a "near-miss" to the table. They are not the one who failed; they are the "engineer" who found the broken wrench *before* it broke the entire machine.

3. **Ask "Why," Not "Who":** When a failure is found, you must forbid the question "Who did this?" Instead, you ask a series of "Why" questions about the *system*:

- *"Why did our process allow this to happen?"*
- *"Why was the 'buddy system' not in place here?"*
- *"Why was the deadline unclear?"*
- *"Why was the person on this task too burned out to see the error?"*

4. **Make the Fix Public:** The solution is never "This person needs more training." The solution is "We need a new, clear protocol for this task." You then share this new protocol with everyone, so the lesson is only paid for once.

Why It Works:

This system creates profound psychological safety. It changes the incentive structure from hiding (to protect the self) to revealing (to protect the team). When it is safe to be honest, you unlock the collective intelligence of your entire team. You create a group of engineers who are constantly, passionately, and safely upgrading their own system. This is the foundation of a high-performance, resilient culture.

5. Getting in the Mud (The Final Integration)

The Concept:

Ben's journey reveals a final, subtle trap. After mastering his own mind (The Anchor) and learning to support others (The Umbrella), his ego created a new, powerful, and very dangerous costume: The Savior. He became the "Wise Engineer," the calm, all-knowing leader who could fix any problem, be it a broken process or a broken heart. This performance, while "positive," was just another glass office, leaving him admired but completely alone.

The Problem:

The goal of this work is not to become a perfect, calm, unshakable guru. That is just another, colder performance. The goal is to become a whole, messy, authentic human being. We are not meant to float above our lives as a "cloud," observing the chaos from a safe distance. We are meant to be in our lives. We are meant to be in the mud.

The Practice: "Living It, Not Performing It"

This final practice is not a new tool. It is the commitment to stop using the other tools as a way to hide. It is the art of being fully human, anchored in the mess of reality.

1. **Drop the "Fixer" Identity:** When you are with your team, your partner, or your children, your job is not to be the "Savior." Your job is to be a partner. This means you must have the courage to say, "I don't know the answer," or "This is awful, and I don't know what to do, but I'm here with you." Vulnerability is the end of performance.

2. **Join the Emotion (Don't Just Observe It):** When your child is having a tantrum, don't just "observe their storm." Get on the floor, acknowledge their rage, and be silly. When your partner is in pain, don't "diagnose" their story. Just hold them. Connect with the *feeling*, not the *idea* of the feeling.

3. **Use Your Anchor to *Stay*, Not to *Escape*:** The purpose of The Anchor is not to detach you from life; it is to anchor you *in* life. When a crisis hits, you feel your feet on the floor, not to float away, but to stay present and engaged in the chaos without being swept away by it. You are in the mud, but the mud is not in you.

4. **Stop "Trying" to Be Present:** The ultimate goal is to stop "practicing" and just "be." You will not be "Ben the Mindful Leader." You will just be Ben. A man who gets angry, and then apologizes. A man who gets scared, and then acts anyway. A man who is sometimes a brilliant engineer, sometimes a confused husband, and sometimes a silly dad banging a spoon on the floor.

Why It Works:

This is the end of the war with yourself. You stop trying to be a "better version" of yourself and simply embrace the version that is here. You are not a problem to be fixed. You are a person to be lived.

The "roommate" will still talk, the storms will still come, the mud will still be messy. But you will no longer be at war with any of it. You will be anchored in your own imperfect, real, and wonderful life, finally at home, with your hands in the earth.

Discussion Guide for Teams

How to Use This Guide: This book was written to be more than just a story; it was written to start a conversation. Use these questions at your next team offsite, leadership retreat, or book club to move from "reading" the concepts to "living" them.

Part 1: The Mirror (Self-Reflection)

Before we look at the team, we must look at ourselves.

1. **The Roommate:** In the story, Ben realizes he has a "roommate" in his head—a voice that constantly narrates fears about the past (Yesterday) or the future (Tomorrow). How does your own "roommate" show up under pressure? Does it tend to be a "Critic" (telling you you're not enough) or a "Alarmist" (telling you everything is about to collapse)?

2. **The Glass Office:** Ben's glass office represents visibility without connection—people can see him, but they can't reach him. Do you ever feel "lonely at the top" or isolated from your team, even when you are physically present? What behaviors (like checking phones, constant busyness, or closed doors) do we use to keep people at a distance?

3. **The Cloud vs. The Mud:** Ben tries to solve his anxiety by becoming a "Cloud"—calm, detached,

and observant. But Hannah tells him she misses the "jerk in the mud" because at least he was real. In our leadership, do we sometimes over-correct and become too clinical or detached? How can we be calm without being cold?

Part 2: The Team Dynamic (Culture)

Diagnosing the health of our own "41st Floor."

4. **The Anxiety Tax:** Ben's team was paying a heavy "Anxiety Tax"—wasting energy on fear, hiding mistakes, and managing perceptions rather than doing the work. On a scale of 1-10, how high is the "Anxiety Tax" in our current team? What is one thing causing it?

5. **The "Broken Wrench":** When Tom misses the deadline, Kael notes that the "bolt wasn't tightened" because the wrench (the system) was broken, not just the man. Can you identify a recent mistake in our organization that we blamed on a person, but was actually a system failure?

6. **Safety to Speak:** Tom only admitted his error because he felt safe enough to do so. Do our junior team members feel safe enough to bring us a "Code Red" the moment it happens? If not, what specific fear is stopping them?

Part 3: The New Covenant (Action)

Building our own operating system.

7. **The "New Covenant" Protocols:** Ben's team instituted three non-negotiable rules:

- ***The Buddy System:*** *No critical work goes out alone.*
- ***Dark Hours:*** *Mandatory disconnection to prevent burnout.*
- ***Blameless Post-Mortems:*** *Hunting for system flaws, not villains. Which of these three protocols would have the biggest immediate impact on our team if we implemented it tomorrow?*

8. **Redefining "Soft":** When Peters calls the new system "soft," Ben argues it is actually a "fortress" of resilience. Do we view rest and psychological safety as a luxury or as a strategic asset? How does burnout affect our bottom line (errors, turnover, lost creativity)?
9. **The Umbrella:** Maya teaches Ben to "bring an umbrella"—to sit with people in their storm rather than trying to fix it. Who on our team is currently in a "storm"? How can we show up for them as partners rather than just problem-solvers this week?

Team Exercise: The Blameless Post-Mortem

Objective: To practice finding system flaws instead of assigning blame.

Instructions:

1. Identify a "Near-Miss" or a small failure that occurred in the last month.
2. Set a timer for 20 minutes.

3. Rule 1: You are forbidden from using the word "Who."
4. Rule 2: You must ask "Why" five times to get to the root cause (The System).
    - *Why did the error happen?* (Because the deadline was missed.)
    - *Why was the deadline missed?* (Because the team was overloaded.)
    - *Why was the team overloaded?* (Because we took on an un-scoped project.)
    - *Why did we take on an un-scoped project?* (Because we lack a clear intake protocol.)
5. Outcome: Create one specific, new protocol (like Ben's "Buddy System") to fix that root cause.